let me tell you

ALSO BY PAUL GRIFFITHS

on music

A Concise History of Modern Music (1978)
Olivier Messiaen and the Music of Time (1985)
Modern Music and After (1995)
The Sea on Fire: Jean Barraqué (2003)
The Penguin Companion to Classical Music (2004)
The Substance of Things Heard (2005)
A Concise History of Western Music. (2006)

fiction

Myself and Marco Polo (1989)
The Lay of Sir Tristram (1991)

for music

The Jewel Box (music by Mozart, 1991)
What Next? (music by Elliott Carter, 1999)
there is still time (music by Frances-Marie Uitti, 2003)
The General (music by Beethoven, 2007)

let me tell you

paul griffiths

Paul Griffiths

REALITY STREET
2008

Published by
Reality Street Editions
63 All Saints Street, Hastings, East Sussex TN34 3BN
www.realitystreet.co.uk

Printed & bound in Great Britain by CPI Antony Rowe

Reality Street Narrative Series No 6

A catalogue record for this book is available from the British Library

ISBN: 978-1-874400-43-1

for Anne

* * * * * *

READ ME

I do not know, now, how all this will end. You will see, in what follows, what Ophelia will have to say of her life before the start of our play. You will hear her speak of her father, Polonius, and of her brother, Laertes. They were with us all the time, so you will hear her speak of me, of my wife, Gertrude, and of the son Gertrude had with my brother: Hamlet. And all this Ophelia will speak in her own words, those words alone. She is like the rest of us; we all have no more than the words that come to us in the play. We go on with these words. We have to. But if we should break them up, as Ophelia does here, what then? And look: I too have gone from my part. I begin to fear. I have loved my life as it is, say what you will.

— *The King*

1

So: now I come to speak. At last. I will tell you all I know. I was deceived to think I could not do this. I have the powers; I take them here. I have the right. I have the means. My words may be poor, but they will have to do.

What words do I have? Where do they come from? How is it that I speak?

There will be a time for me to think of these things, but right now I have to tell you all that I may of me—of me from when I lay on my father's knees and held up my hand, touching his face, which he had bended down over me. That look in his eyes....

My father.

Well, I have done what I could. And I believe, by now, I have done *all* that I could. That's the reason there's this difference in me now, that I may speak my thoughts as I wish.

Still, it's hard. I see that face of his. What would *he* wish me to do?

That face. What does it say?

There may be some will tell me I cannot remember from being so little, and they may be right. Some of these may be false remembrances, things my father would say to me, and say again, time upon time, as was his way, so that I think I remember them. I must do all I may to find from them what is truly mine, now that I have made up my mind to speak to you like this.

There are so many of these things. It's as if I held a glass in my hand and could see them all, there in the glass, the things I remember, remembrances all tumbled one upon another, some before they should be, some late, all out of time—the sun over the cold green mountain, a scholar with a hard look in his eyes, my father shaking as he rose to give a speech, my brother with flowers in his hand and he would not say what for, a lost sandal, a music lesson—and it's up to me to be patient and lay them down the right way.

There are things, as well, I do not see, things that come to me as speech, and some as music. A call.

'O, please come now! Now!'

Is this my father? No.

'O, how long must I be down here without you?'

I see the young me, up the cold green mountain, down on the grass, one hand on—what is it?—some little herb. And still that call. She cannot let me be.

'O, come now! Right away! You should be here with me!'

I lay still. It's as if I was held by what was in my hand, by what my hand was touching. It's as if I had been locked there, locked to the mountain, with my eyes quite still, on my hand and the herb in the grass. And all the powers in hell could not have made me go from there.

But I, such a little nothing as I was, I could make me go—did make me go.

'O, *now*! Do you—?'

She—this young me—I see look up, but not at these words. My arm rises to keep my eyes from the sun. I see it. This is indeed as it was. I remember. An arm rises to the sun, a head from what thoughts it had, two knees from the grass. There was that call, but it seemed to come from a long way away, whilst in my head was another call, no words this time—the call of my thoughts. What should I do? Which path should I take? This way, that way?

‘O, please, you cannot go away by yourself!’

I look at me now as I was then. This is like being one of my own observers, but with no powers over what is observed. It all must go as it does. All I may do is see what this little I will do. I look in the glass to do so: I raised my head. My hand let go the herb. I have gone, down the mountain. I have gone.

What was I then? Two? Two up the mountain, two as this little I goes down the mountain with a good grace, as she answers the call that had come?

Let time be turned from here. Let these little treads I make down the mountain go up again, restore that right hand to the herb it held, that head to the patient perusal it made. Let little I be there again in the grass, and from here go on and on to before all this, to where she—I—had come from.

This is it. Let me go right away, now, whilst it is still not late, to before all this—to before the mountain and the unbraced out-doors and the little me in it all, with my hand touching the herb and my head in the heavens, to before the time these eyes of mine look up, as I see them look up now, to before that last call to come in.

‘O, that’s right! Come here. Down to me. See what I have for you.’

Do not fear: that’s what I would say to this little me now. The time will come when you do not have to go down there, when you do not have to do what she will ask, when you may please yourself.

This is it, now, that time. It’s come.

So let’s go on to before, all the way to the end of my memory, to what was for me Day One. Let’s come to that day she bore me, the day I draw breath.

It's like this. It is morning. The sun is pale; it's a cold morning.

There she is, on the bed. She does not look at the window, to the sun, but away, to the door, as if in expectation that some one would come in. I see all this, for some reason, as if from by the window.

There's another one there. Right. My father. The pale morning sun stole from the window over the bed and over the bed clothes, and now it falls in my memory on them: she on the bed, my father, and no doubt another they would have had there to be a help.

He—my father—could never keep still. He comes and goes from one end of the chamber to the other—one way, then the other, his eyes down. And she, she does not look at him but still at the door, never but at the door. They do not speak. There is no more than this: his treads on the stone, up and down.

But let all this go, for how could I remember this day? How could I remember a time when I was not?

I have to think more before I go on like this. False memory may speak, I find, as well as true. I have to know the difference. And I have to see to it that I do not make things up. It's hard. Indeed, it may well seem hard for all of us, to know what it is that we truly know—and what it is that we know to be true. Another difference, it may be. There is more in my mind than I know. I must look hard at what comes to me, cast away the grass and keep the flowers.

I know I have it in me to say things that are not so and have never been so, but that I wish had been so. There are, as well, things in my head that I cannot remember and never will remember. They are not in my memory; they are in me.

But now and again words come to me as if it rained words in my head—words given me by some other, as if I had no hand in what I say, as if all I may do is give speech, let the words come and come, and go on and on, and whilst they go on I cannot say what I would truly wish to say. I may do nothing, held still by my own words—if they are my own. My words go on, but *I* cannot speak.

I have to make it so that my face cannot speak without my mind, that my words do not take form other than as I wish.

I will do so. Mark my words.

So on with it. That mountain: it was a green sandal loosed from the heels of heaven.

I remember it well. My hand touching that herb. A shirt, held out of a window, shaking in the morning sun. The way the maid's head was raised as if to sing, but then she goes on with the sewing. And over all the cold green mountain.

Each morning the sun would come up over the mountain, and we would pray, my father and I, and then with my brother as well, pray for a good day, and pray at the end of the day for a good night.

This was when *she* had gone. She left when I was little, but that's one of the things I'll come to. If things still come out of my jangled memory here and there before they should, that could be for woe, but then again it could be for joy—if not for the two, hand in hand. But I will do all I may to have things right from here on.

The day I have to find in my memory now is

another day, and a day of joy this one was, the day when I was given my brother.

This is something I do indeed remember—and this is where that false memory comes from, of the one on the bed, and the pale morning sun, and the bed clothes, and the head turned away, and my father as he made his way up and down.

I would have been still little when she bore him, but more than I was in that other memory, of being up the mountain.

As I remember, hard as this may be to believe, I was there, there on the bed, my little hand touching that face. She and I. (This is not something I like to remember at all. That means it must be true.)

And no, my father was not there. There must have been other treads of his that go on in my mind.

My father was not with us for some reason. It could be that he had to be with His Majesty that morning, for—and no doubt it would have been better to say this before—he was one of the king's right-hand men. He was at the king's call, day and night. He is now, he is still. Do this, do that.

But no, it's not quite like that. My father is the king's shoulder: that's how it is. The two of them know each other so well that my father does not have to think what the king will say. Indeed, he could almost speak for the king, and the day may come when he will have to, if the king's not better before long.

So it was with the king as was, at the time I now speak of, that my father was held in honour and had to go all over for him. Then we, my brother and I, would have to do without him whilst he was away. She, at such a time, was the one we had to go to.

But again I go on before I should. I'll come to all this, of my father, and the counsel he would give the king—the king as was and the king we have now. This will all come out at the right time.

As for now, there we are, on the bed in the pale morning: she and me. That's what I remember. That's how it was.

No, that's still not right, cannot be. There was another. I have it. The maid. The maid's here with us as well, by the bed. How could I not remember that the maid was there?

And then there he was: my brother. The maid took him up by the heels. I see this. To me he had a puffed-up look—'bonny', the maid would say. He sucked in one breath, and with that my love, little as I was. He did not weep, not at all, but let out something like a little moan, as if—so it seemed to me—he could say 'O'. And he turned his eyes to look at me.

So now there are two of us. That's good. It was good not to be by yourself with such a one as she was. We had each other now. My brother and I had each other.

The maid held him—my brother—close with one hand before she had to lay him down on the bed. There I could look and look at him.

Then she took him away again, to redeliver him to us in a long shirt (the one they would christen him in). Now he was right by me. I remember a little ankle, remember touching a little ankle. I remember touching his face with my tongue.

He was still. All was still. All is still.

And out of that still morning I seem to remember how

the maid would sing to us. Was it then? Most of the time she would sing to us at night, as she took us to bed.

There was a lady all in green,
Nony the nony no no,
Was locked away and was not seen,
Nony the nony no no.
Quoth she: 'I cannot find my tear,
The tear that falls each morning here,
The tear of grace, the tear of fear,
The tear that falls upon the bier',
Nony the nony no no.

A young lord by the window stayed,
Nony the nony no no,
And bended to this speech she made,
Nony the nony no no.
He left that day to find the tear,
The tear of grace, the tear of fear,
The tear that falls each morning here,
The tear that falls upon the bier,
Nony the nony no no.

He did not look down to the grass,
Nony the nony no no,
He did not see the rose of glass,
Nony the nony no no.
The rose of grace, the rose of fear,
The rose that falls each morning here,
The rose of glass that was the tear,
The rose that falls upon the bier,
Nony the nony no no.

There's more I have to say of the maid—more I would wish to say of the maid—and let me say it now here, all of it.

She was not young. But to a little one that means nothing. What meant all to us was that, without being quite one of us, she was with us. If there was one lesson we took from the maid, it was to know what you are—to know what you are in yourself, and how to find it. She did not take a command well, not from me and not from my brother. Never. But if you would ask, there was nothing she would not do for you.

She honoured my father.

What she may have been like to the other when no-one was there with them, I do not know.

To us two, my brother and I.... Well, she blasted us with love, day upon day.

She held us, one in each arm, and held us to each other. She would look down at us and say nothing—say nothing but look and look, harsh with love.

I remember that breath on my face. I remember that look: harsh indeed, but sweet as well. And the more I think of it, what I remember most of all is a long-lost perfume: the perfume of being held, of clothes on my face.

This is the maid, in my memory, as she was, the one that held us. She comes from some way away, from over the mountain. She does what she must, and more. Nothing does she say, not to us, most of the time. But we look as she goes from one chamber to another. We do not know if she'll mind that she's being observed: we are young and do not think of that. And if she does know we are there, she does not let on. We go where she goes. We, that know what it is to be patient observers, look on as she does what she does.

She would go to the well each morning. I see a hard cold hand.

On the day when the baker would come to the door, she would ask us what we would wish for—'wish for', she would say. Ask us, not my father, and not the other.

We would go to see them at the door, my brother and I. We would look at them, the maid and the baker, for as long as they stayed there. We could not tell, from where we lay, what these two would say to each other. But we could see. There would be a difference in the maid's face.

Other things.

She did not blame us when it rained and a glass of pansies (I think) by the window—indeed, pansies they must have been, from by the path—was blown over.

She took us out one night to see an owl. My father did not know of this. She did not tell us what we would see, but raised a hand to show us the owl, pale in the night like a saint.

When she *did* speak, it was in the way of over the mountain. 'See' would be more like 'say', and 'say' like 'sigh'. 'Fair' and 'fare' would be more like 'fear'. There was, as well, something hard in this breath-cast speech. It was as if she did not wish to speak, longed never to speak at all, and so words—when indeed words would come—would have to come out all at one go.

One day we, my brother and me, made it seem we had lost all powers of speech and would have to speak by means of letters. (When you are little you do these things.) I remember how, at the table, with my brother close by, I held that hard cold hand to help the maid form some words. Little madam that I was!

But the 'A' she made was more like an 'S', and my brother had to say 'No, that's not it at all', and right away she was up from the table, and the lesson had come to an end.

That look as she left: I see it now.

She was no beauty, not at all, but to me she was beauteous—to me and to my brother. Beauteous: it's one of the words that, to me, goes with the maid and no other. And beauteous she must have been to the baker, for there comes the day when she goes away with him, over the mountain again. She did not tell us she was to go. Did she think that, had she done so, she could have been stayed by us, held there by us? We go down one morning to find she's gone. That was that.

It was a late love for the two of them. It was a love we had observed but not seen. It was a love that was for them, for the two of them, of each for the other, not for us to know.

As I think of the maid, the remembrances come one upon another: a look that could say more than words, a hand on my arm. And this: the grace that made, I will now say, a home.

2

Let me come to another day—another day that is not like this one now, where time goes on, and I have to say what I may whilst I still may do so, for I do not know what time I have.

But there, in my memory, time is still.

Here, here as I speak, I know what it is to be me: to be one, on my own. There I have to find this other me, the one I was—which means there are two: me now and me then. Indeed, there may be more: a chorus of me, the observed and the observers. Here the day may go as it will—and all I may do is hope it will go well. There, there in the glass, it is done. It's all over.

No, it's not over as long as I have not done with it. It's stayed. There may be more to it than I have seen. Many things have stayed in that way: the day I lost my way up the mountain when I turned from the path; the day I promised my father I would see to some form for him and then did not do it—so many things that it's hard for me to know which should come before another.

And then there are the things I would see time and again, so that they seem in my memory to make up one day—one day that turned like a wheel.

Is this no more than the effect of memory, that one day will seem like another? No, for the young this is how it is. Time then did not go on. All was before you, still to come. No one left. Nothing was lost for good. And what was death?

Each morning I see the maid on the way to the well.

Each morning my brother rises from his little bed and comes to me in mine.

Each morning what my brother and I have to say to each other, him and then me, is what's come to us in the night. A king with a withered arm. Another king with one good daughter and two that are not. The table turned on an ungartered steward.

Each morning we have to be patient—but never with each other. No, being with each other was not hard. We had to be patient before the time when my father could see us. So we stayed in bed. Then my father would come to the door.

Each morning, in bed, the words tumbled on and on as we tumbled over each other, and then more as we lay quite still.

'I was up the mountain and there was a bed of flowers by the path, you know. There was a rose with the face of a lady, but she did not speak. I could see long columbines with eyes all their length, but I do not think they could see me. And some pansies, like there are. I had gone to take one up and, touching it, it made me cold all over, and I took a look down at my hand, and it had turned my hand green.'

I see this now as I could see it then. I look as my hand becomes a dove, a green dove, and is loosed from my arm, and goes up and away. And then I look again, and my hand is as it was.

'Are they all down on the ground?'

'What?'

'The flowers.'

'No.'

'So what made you say they lay in bed?'

Then each morning we would go down to be with them—my father and *she* and the maid: two at the table, with us two, whilst the maid does things for us.

Each morning we have to see what we have seen before—each morning, that is, before the day *she* left.

If my father was not there, the maid would call us down, and it would be us and the other one at the table. The maid would come to us with a glass in each hand—one for my brother, one for me—and say nothing. The other one would say nothing. So it would go on. The maid, with nothing now to do, would go to the window and look out at the mountain.

When my father is there and the two of them are at the table, they say 'Good morning' as we come in, and we say 'Good morning' as well. That's all. Then, as the maid does what she must, *she*, the other one, goes on with that way she had, that perusal of my father, and he goes on as if there's nothing in it. When all's done we go out.

We go out. My brother was two by now, and I held him by the hand as we took the path up the mountain—right up to the brow, for it seemed to us we had to go all the way up before we could play.

It was not that we did not wish for them to know what we did. By no means. There was nothing of that in it. But we had to be away. That was all.

At the brow of the mountain we stayed, and did not go down before the morning was quite over.

It's all here, in my mind, right as it was. I could be lost in it, and not come away. But I will.

He was sweet in his sun hat.

We stayed, as I say, at the brow of the mountain. There we are.

I look at him. He had a hand raised over his eyes.

He does not know what I will do. How could he? I

did not know. And I did not know at the time what made me do what I did. But I think I know now. We had come from that table, from the two that had nothing to say to each other.

I took my right arm. I sucked and sucked at it.

He made a little moan, as before. It turned out to be a way he had when there was something he could not do with.

But I had to go on: there was something I had to show him. I did not know what, but there was something I had to show him, here and now.

It does not go right. I see him weep. Tear on tear falls hard from his eyes. The mountain grass was bewept.

My arm falls and I draw to him a little, but without quite touching. I do not know what to do.

There we are, not quite touching. My hand is not quite on his shoulder. But still, his little weep and his moan are over. His eyes are on me, as they had been before, all the time.

Then I show him my arm. There is a mark on my arm. It rises as we look.

And there is the sun, and there is the mountain: all where we are is in an ecstasy of expectation.

We look at the mark on my arm—his eyes and mine, on that mark. Then we look at each other. There is nothing to say.

I see us go down again, hand in hand.

It's not like that now. Now he's away on his own, my brother, his hand, I know, in another's. And that's good. That's as it should be.

But it must be from him, from being with him, that

I have come to know how good, how right, it is to find a hand in mine, not locked but loosed there, touching. There's a difference now, as I do not have to say. Still, here on the brow of the mountain, with my little brother, this is, I believe, where I find what it's like to have a hand in my own, find how it would please me—the joy it would give me to know that some other is truly there, with me, as close as a hand's touching.

A hand is affection. A hand is honour. A hand is honesty.

A hand is mercy, the hand of one to another, a hand to help.

It is holy, the touching of a hand.

A hand given is one of the gifts of the heart.

A hand may say this: 'I will be with you, from now to the end of time. I will never let you go. You will think of me as your own. I will be your own.'

A hand may be an argument to them that do not believe in love.

'Here is my hand', one will say. 'This is my hand. I give you my hand.' There's nothing I may give you that means more.

'I take your hand', the other will say. 'I have your hand in mine.' There's nothing I may take from you that means more. 'And in being like that with you, I have given you my hand. This is my hand. This is me.'

Here: I have held it out to you. Take my hand. Go with me. Be with me.

Not all remembrances are good to restore to the mind. I'll come again to my brother and me on the mountain, how we would go there in the sun to play. But for now let me go on.

Months have gone by from the morning of the mark on my arm. No-one other than us, my brother and I, had given it a look—no, not the maid. I did not like to keep things from the maid, but this time I had to, so it seemed to me. And my brother, so young, could say nothing of what had gone on. That was a help, in a way. In another way it was not. The shame was more.

Morning upon morning, when in bed with me, he had come and held my arm to his face, touching where the mark was to his face. That was all. He would have it so, my arm held to his face, his little hand on it as we lay there. Nothing did we say to one another. And we could see the mark go down.

Then there had to come the time when they would not let us play all day long. Before we could go out we had to do the morning's lesson, which would be in commerce, letters, music and so on.

Two men would come each morning to give us the lesson of the day. One of them had a way of touching his tongue with his hand when he had to think. The other was pale and grave of feature, and had the look of a courtier that had been denied something.

They do not come now—indeed, they have not come for a long time—but they are still here close by, and I see them now and then. They do not seem to know me. They go by without a look.

I cannot say I mind: I could never find a way to like them. But still, they are good men. And over the months we had with them—months and months, lesson upon lesson—they did what they had come to do. I have to say that. There we would all be, day in, day out, and they would speak to us, of this, that and the other. Most of the time my brother and I would say nothing: there was no expectation that we would. They did not ask for my thoughts, and they did not ask for my brother's. But we would find we had come to know things we did not know before.

Not all of these things have stayed with me. Indeed, I wish I could remember more from that morning lesson we would have each day. As it is, what's left to me is a little here and there—things it would be hard to call 'memory'.

But let me see what I may call to mind.

Naught, one, two, and so on. Naught. How I would find it hard to believe in that naught! Still do. Nothing. But nothing as something, something you call naught. So not nothing at all. There is no nothing. Nothing is something. Naught. O.

And music. Let me say here all that I know of music: it will not take long.

The late king composed—the king that died by his own hand, as some say, but that's another of the things I'll come to. Indeed he did, composed—with no other to help him—things he had some of us do each Valentine's Day as a charity show: I was in more than one of them. *The Honourable Libertine, Other Pastors, Tenders Tomorrow, Never Love a Scholar*—and all with his own words, musicked by himself. He was quite something—in what he would go for, you had to give him that. One must say. I was not that keen on most of his music; still, I could not but see what it meant to him.

And he composed chamber music as well. There was a tune in the key of A—the key of love, I believe. Now, that was something that's stayed in my mind. It was a tune my father would like to play, and I would ask him to play it again, and he would make as if to do so, his hand raised, but he could never play it twice, it made him weep so. That was the effect on him. To me it seemed sweet, that tune. To him there was more to it. I never could find out quite what. But then, I did not ask.

More of these things come to me. *Beauty's Argument, The Two Noble Watchmen, Better Believe It!* This last was poor, to my mind. But I was on my own in that: it was held to be good by most observers, I have to say, and for some it was right at the head of the king's music. They remember it still. Better believe it.

There's something in one of these things of the king's: I cannot remember which, but it was not that one, I know. It's a tune that's almost like 'Remember Me', but not quite. The chorus goes like this:

O, but no. I cannot sing. I cannot sing, not now. That time is over and done with. Music died here: it died when the late king died. It is no more. It's gone for good.

If you wish to have music, you must tear yourself away and go from here. Here all is still, still as night. We do not have the joy of music.

It's as if a robin rises and there's nothing. It's as if a glass falls and there's nothing. That's the way of it.

There was a time when I could sing, and then I would sing and sing. My father would love to have me sing to him, at the end of a hard day. But that's all over. Now he would say, if one should ask, that he's no time for music. And what is music if not time: time of now and then tumbled in to one another, time turned and loosed, time sweet and harsh, flowers of time?

But to go on with what I still know of the music

that was here of late, no other but the king composed for us. His was all the music we had, such as it was.

I know I must seem to say little of his stature, but he left us all, I think, with the wish that we could have had other music, if no more than for the difference of it. Difference is good: each becomes better than it was, if there's some play of one with another. So, whilst I did, come to think, quite like some of the king's things, I would wish there had been other music. Now I wish there could be *some* music.

There was a time when I would play as well as sing, and play quite well, I think. But it never seemed to me I could have composed. Music was something given.

Then music was something given *up*. But no, it was more as if music had given us up.

Me-la-so, I seem to remember—remember, it would seem, from so long a time—, *la-so-me*. But what this means to me now is no more than words, little words, and words without a tune.

It's like this. These of us that are still here—and I think I may speak for all of us in this—have lost the affection we had for music. That's hard. Without affection music means nothing. It is cold thoughts and form. It is snow on your grave. It is a soldier that treads on the snow on your grave. One, two. One, two. One, two.

That's all I know of music. That's all I remember of music.

My brother could play better than I could—and sing as well, but it was hard to make him. Still, there was one lesson where I was better than him by a long way, which was when we had to speak in another tongue.

I would give him what help I could. '*Do-no*' I would say, to show the right length of each 'o'. I give. You, my brother, give. He, my master, will give. She is given. We are the givers. They should have had the gifts. These could not have been the gifts that should have been given.

Now and again my father would help us in this when he had been away for the king. So did my father's brother one time. He, like my father, was on the king's staff.

He was a good soul, so like my father in many things. I say 'was', for he is no more with us, alas: he died a little before the late king, and on that day (I see it now), as we lay him in the ground up there, the sun comes out, and it seems the mountain rises a little to close over him. I remember how he held us, my brother and me, one on each of his knees, as he would tell us what he had seen whilst he was away. And we would be touching his beard. My father did not have a beard at that time, so his brother's beard—which was like snow—was something I could not take my eyes away from. So it was with my little brother. There we would be, each of us with a hand in it. You would think that would have made it hard for him to speak, but he let us be. And we would look at him, look at his beard, see it shaking a little with his breath—the breath that was on my brother's hand as it was on mine.

There was a time he had come over-night from Givers-la-Rède, and took us on his knees to say this:

'My my, I think they are all pansies over there, you know. Nothing means more to them than fashion. I took the coach to where the Sun King made his home. Chamber upon chamber upon chamber, all with glass doors. Quite good. But no baker there could make what we have at home. Nothing like.'

And here I could see him look at the maid. But she stayed bended down sewing, as if she would give him no mind. That was how they had been with each other from long before. How could she speak from the heart when this was the master's brother? And he, how could he show his hand?

My father was there this time, the other not. That would be the way of it.

'I had to have many a lesson in how they speak,' he goes on, 'before I could go and whilst I was there as well. Would you like me to tell you something of it?'

And how could we say no?

'*Non* means *no*.'

I think: My brother, little as he is, does not find these things so hard he could not have done that one for himself. I look over at him. He, like me, still had his hand in that snow-beard, and he does not look my way. I say nothing. No more does he. We are of one mind on that. No one could be unkind to Gis.

Then, with the beard now still, we see that the time's come for one of us to say something, ask something. I look at my brother again. He's shaking his head a little. Then I speak.

'What's the most you may say then, Gis?'

At this good Gis stayed down in his thoughts a little—down, but with his eyes up to think.

'Well, my little two,'—he would call us this, his 'little two'—'I'll give this a go. Let's see how many words I may remember if I think hard. Right.'

Then he turned to look at us, from one to the other.

'La rue Saint-Valentine, long, a if à but; la rose pâle me face à la table.'

'Good heavens, that's something', I say: no doubt this would have come from my father's way of speech. 'Let's have it again.'

'La rue Saint-Valentine, long, a if à but; la rose pâle me face à la table. O la la, o la la.'

So it goes, this time with a little tune at the end.

That means it's over to me again. What shall I say? Then it comes to me: ask him if he had another tongue he could speak in.

Gis cast his eyes down. Did I know there was something not quite right here? Did I know what this would have raised up in his mind?

I believe not. There would be another day, another time, when Gis would tell us of the time when he was a soldier a long way from home, how he had held one of his men as he died, and 'they did not tell us how to lay out the dead'.

As for now, he let us down from his knees. Was it over? I took a look at him, then at my brother, with his eyes still on Gis. I held out my hand, which my brother took, but he could not let go of Gis with his eyes. I turned away a little, to draw him with me, and as he turned as well, Gis took us again with his words.

'*O arm' Held in See*'—the way he does this is with me still: it's like music, as if he would speak and sing at the one time—

O arm' Held in See,
So hat hell' Bier in Hand,
So is't all's Form an End.

I look at him: there's a tear in his eye, and his mind must be with this *'arm' Held'*—this poor soldier, as I was to find out, this soldier all on his own, his day long over, but this soldier that still stayed where he was, and did not close his eyes to the night of nothing.

3

Now and again the maid would go away, over the mountain, to see the daughter she had—the daughter that was all this time with the maid's brother. (This was before the maid left to go away for good with the baker, at which time he took the daughter as his own.) As I remember, she would go for the night and be with us again late in the morning. Then she would let some months go by before she would go again.

As a little one I did not like it when she was gone. When I rose in the morning there would be something I could not quite remember—did not wish to remember. Then I would. And I fear I took it out on my brother. I did not wish to have him come in then, and he would know that. He did not ask me to play. I would go down without him to the door, which had a window in it. And there, for as long as the maid was gone, I stayed to see when she would come down the mountain again to be with us. Then at last, when I could see the maid, I would be up and away.

'The maid is here, the maid is here', I would say over and over, like a little tune, as I made my way up the mountain, up to the maid, so that we could come down again hand in hand.

There must have been many a time like that. This was one: I had seen the maid come over the brow of the mountain and had gone out, my head raised and my heart with it.

It was a harsh cold day. On the turf to the right of the path, all the flowers had been blown down, and there was no sun. But I did not mind.

'The maid is here, the maid is here. The maid is here, the maid is here.'

So I come now to the maid on the path, and she comes to me, one arm held out, whilst in the other she had the things she took.

I take that hand I know so well in mine and we look at each other as she comes down close to me. She does not have to ask how things have been.

We stayed there, on and on, with me held by that arm on my shoulder, and she bended over to me, as if we did not wish to go home. For me this *was* home, to be with the maid, for as long as she held me. This—I say it again—was what made home. This and my brother. But with my brother, it was more that I made a home for him. That was what the maid did for me. My father could not: he had his own things to do, and he would go away for months at a time, so that I could not think of him that way. The heart of what made a home was the maid. There was no door we had to go in. Home could be out on the mountain—out on the blown grass, as it was here, when I was held by the maid.

I draw away a little, and the maid's hand falls from me.

'Did you find your daughter in good form?' I ask, as I look away. My hope is to say something that means little, but I know right away the words have not come out right. They never do, with the maid and me. It's better if we do not speak, for all that we have to say may be done without words. Words are in the way. And these words of mine come out as if she and I had not been close at all.

The maid's are no better. The effect they make is

indeed of a maid, of one that must do and be what the master's daughter will ask. This is not how it is with us. But we cannot find the words for what we are.

'Ay, she's quite t' young lady now, my love, thank you. All she will think of, would you believe, is fashion, from morning to night. There was a feature in one of them Sundays on Christian.... Nay, I cannot remember on Christian what. Christian this, Christian that: there are so many Christians. And these things never meant nothing to me, I have to say. But she...!'

'Clothes?' I say. 'What does she like? You must take some of mine to your daughter, by all means, please. I have so many.'

And indeed I had. *She* let me have all I could wish for. In all honesty I have to say she did that for me.

But there may have been something in this I could not see: it may not have been done for me at all. In all she did there would be some other reason. Nothing was as it seemed.

My clothes. I remember a shirt with bells on the right arm; a pale green stole dupped with columbines; stockings, stockings, stockings, in my closet and all over my chamber; a doublet made for me, of wax may-flowers and owl down, which I donned for a play; a long sandal—one long sandal, for I had lost the other one.

'Nay, my love,'—for so she would call me, most of all when she had been away—'give o'er. You are good, but I would not wish this daughter of mine more puffed-up than 'a' is. Keep what th'hadst. Belike she'll then come to know what she is and what she comes from. That'll be hard, I know, but she must.'

That was all she would say. End of speech. If I

should ask again what I could find for that daughter, she would say nothing to me. I know that. She never answers again when she's had to say no, so I give up.

Did she, another day, say more of this daughter? I cannot remember so well, but no, I think not. And there had still been nothing more by the day she took me (my brother was not with us) over the mountain to where the daughter was.

Over the mountain we have gone, without two words to say, all morning long. That's how it should be: we are on the right path with each other now.

Before we left she did, I remember, ask me if I would like to go. 'Will you come with me this time?' That was all she had to say. 'Indeed I will.' She had my things, for she would know she had but to ask. So we left.

And there: from up over the brow of the mountain we could see it. We had turned, and there it was, quite close down there, where the maid's brother's tumbled-down little home was.

I see the maid now. She treads down the steep path, and so do I, down to the door. She goes before me. We go one by one, in tune with each other.

Late that night, when I was in bed, in a chamber all my own, I lay with my eyes on the door.

At home the maid would come in each night to see that I was all right, but on this night, with a brother and a daughter to keep in mind, she was late. And she did not seem so composed. She had a deject look, as if there was something she had to tell me but did not wish to.

She stayed by the door. I think she will speak from

there, but then she comes over to my bed. When I was little and had a cold she would come in bed with me. This she does not do now, but, bended down, with a hand on my arm, she is there by me, still with that look. Then out it comes, this long speech she seemed to know by heart, almost as if she had done it before, and that goes on and on, words she had to tell me. I remember it all: when she did it, how she did it, and what she had to say.

As to the how, she did not speak this time the way she did most of the time, the over-the-mountain way, but more like us. I did not think of this right then, but it could be she had been given this long speech by my father. I could see this, the two of them in his morning chamber, where she would have to say it over and over to him, like a lesson, so he would know she had it right. But if so, what reason could he have had not to tell me all this himself? I cannot think.

As to the what, here it is:

'Words are what he will say.

' "Words" is what he will say.

' "Words, words, words."

'He'll say this to your father, when the two of them are with each other, and—as he must think—no other is there with them. Never for a breath must he know that the king is close by as well, out of the way.

'What more do we know of him? That he's a scholar. That his shirt is like night. That he's a little ungracious now and then. Do I have to say more? That his father was—at the time we speak of—the king of Denmark. Now do you know him? That his father's brother is the king of Denmark. (Indeed it is so. This is the way it will have turned out.) That you will have seen him, over the months of death and joy there will have been by then—for all this will come—, worse than he was and better than he will be. That in his face there's something of his soul—something of such cold woe that one could weep. That he is, as we speak, not one of the dead. Death will come to him, as to us all—as to, I should say, many of us. Not all. Not quite all.'

This I have had come to mind again and again. I know that what she had to say to me here was a way to counsel me, if I could but make it out. But there are many things that I never have made out—and this last most of all. For death cannot be deceived. Death comes not to 'many of us' but indeed to all—if not, then there will have to be an end before death.

I think of what this other end could be, the end that is not death, the end that is before death, the end that may, then, have loosed us from death, should we have that grace.

The end, the end.

The more I think of these words of the maid's, the more I wish she had had more to say that night. At the time I did not think to ask for more: it did not seem it was mine to ask, but to receive. But I ask now.

Which of us will not have to see death? What becomes of them that have not died at the end? What, indeed, is the end if not death? Where may we go other than to flowers and the bier, with pastors to pray for us, bewept by all and by bells?

You see, my own words give me reason for doubt. I have these words that keep thoughts of death in my mind, an expectancy I cannot repel, but which rises up again and again, and I have to draw hard away from it.

No more of that. Please.

It is as if my own words could tell me, before the time, of my death. This is the reason I think there will not be an end for me that is not death. This is the reason I believe I will be one of the dead, one of the died and gone, like grass, when the end comes. So I do not have to mind what that other end will be. It will not come for me. There will be no end but death, death that comes in pale clothes.

No.

I say no to death. But what is my 'no' to this pale being that will come to take me with him? Will he let me go?

I hope my father will not see death. I hope he will go on to find that other end—as it would be, over the mountain of death, if not before that mountain. And my brother. I wish I could know this, could find it out from their words.

Please, no more.

If the maid is right, they will be dead before the end. I wish I could say no for them as well, for all that my own words seem to speak of death.

But do I long for death and not know it? Is that what my words tell me? I think of something Gis would sing, when we had music, something that's stayed with me all this time, from Gis with his beard of snow.

All will come to their own last breath,
Lady, lord and scholar.
All will know the hand of death,
It may be tomorrow.

For what reason are these things locked in my mind

and not other things? May I let them out? If I have indeed longed for death, may I now not do so? What powers do I have to think another way, find another mind for my own, find other words?

No more, I say. I have stayed over-long from what the maid had to say that night. No more of my words, then, but the maid's:

'No, my love, death will not come to us all, but to him it will—death, it may be, in the form of his father, a death he will have sucked in to himself, a death he will play for.

'Some other scholar will tell him of his father, the late king, as seen by a soldier, at night.

'He will go up and out there at night to see for himself, to see his father, and will speak to his father, and his father will speak to him.

'His father will tell him things that have been in his own thoughts, from months before, from the time his father died. (You will remember that time: we will all of us be there at the grave.)'

Indeed it was so. It rained and rained. We stayed whilst the state pastors raised their eyes to pray, one of them touching the shoulder of the dead king's lady (now the king's lady again) with a cold hand, from which she turned away as well as she could.

'We remember before God the soul of this late departed brother, in the hope and expectation that the heavens will receive him, and on the last day, when all will come before their heavenly sovereign....'

But these are words of death again, of which I wish for no more. They are not the maid's, which go on:

'Some time on from then, when the king is there (the brother of the king as now is: you know, the one that had his arm in a cast), the lady will ask him to wear other clothes, but he will not do so, and never does.

'The king will receive and command, as a king should.

'Two men will come to the youth—to the one that had the late king for a father—and each of them will be another scholar again, like him and the one before. If you could take a look at them—see them as they are, right now—you could well think they wish for nothing but to please him. He'll know better.

'What will truly please him will be the men that come to do a play. He'll know them from before. He'll have one of them redeliver a speech, which your father will not like, but for one of the words.

'He, the young lord as he is by now, will then have them give their play—but with a speech that he's made up for one of them—before the king, the lady and many another: indeed, almost all of you. Not me, as I do not have to say. But you'll be there. This is when you are a young lady. You'll be there, as will he—he'll play with you at the play. With you and with the king. More with the king.

'The king's hand will be held up. The play will be stayed by the king, for some reason. The king will go out, call for something, and draw you all with him. You'll not know the king's reason for what he does. No-one will. But you'll all think and you'll all fear.

'What was in the play? Was something meant that you had not seen? You'll go over the words of the play in your mind—you and all of them.

'You'll wish you could have seen more of it, but it does not go on to the end. Not this one.

'So the king rises. The play is over. He'll call out some command.

'He, your young lord again, will see the king on his knees. He'll do nothing. When the time comes for him to do something, he will not. He'll do it tomorrow, so he'll tell himself. Take it from me: tomorrow never comes.

'He'll see the lady in a bed chamber, and speak harsh words. His father will come again, and he'll see him, and speak with him, but the lady will not.

'The king will have him go away, with letters that ask for him to be done away with, but he'll see these letters and give them other words, so it'll be the two that are with him that'll end up dead. These are the two that turned up before, the two he'll have come to know when he went away to be a scholar. This was another lesson for them. I think you know them: they come to play now and again, with you, your brother and the young lord.

'He'll come again to Denmark, and find two other men. They could be, I think, the two from before, them with the letters, but in other clothes. You see, my love, there's more to this than I know of. I do not know what death means here, where the dead may come again—some of them. It may be that I should not say all this to you now, and I would not say it at all if there had been another way, but there is not. You have to know.'

Again words that have stayed in my mind: 'I do not know what death means here.' But it means what it meant for all time, does it not? There is no other death than death. Death is one.

There must be a reason I remember all this. Something here will have to help me.

But I have turned away from the maid's words again, and this time from fear. There are words now that meant more to me than I could quite take in.

'They'll be at a grave.'

She did not say so, but I know this will be *my* grave. There was something of this in my mind at the time, and it comes to my thoughts again and again. How could it not? Do what I may, I cannot make it go away. I will be dead. I will be dead and in my shroud—another of these wretched words I cannot let go of.

If this is not to be, then I have to do something before my time comes. This is the reason for the maid's speech, to tell me that I have to do something if I wish to go on, if I wish to find another path, other words to speak than these words of death.

But they all wish me to be here. I have to be in it with them. As for me, I cannot let them go. How would it be if I left my father, my brother? What would they do? And there's more that I have no wish to be gone from, to have lost to me with no way to restore it. This is where I have my being. This is all I know.

Still, the more I think of these things, the more I know that I would be dead if I stayed here, and which of us could wish for that? There must be some other way, and one day I will find it. All I may do then is hope that all will go well for my father and brother when I have gone. If I stayed I would never know, and if I go I'll never know.

'A master of fashion, with a hat, will come to the

young lord from the king, and ask him to take up his sword in commerce of dalliance with your brother.

'In this your brother will come to his death—'

No.

'—and, as he does so, he'll give the young lord reason at last to let his sword find the king. That it will do. The king, as well, will come to his death, and not before time, for by then his lady, she will be dead. Indeed, this is how it is. The lady's death—'

All this death.

'—is what will have made him, the young lord—when he had long denied himself this, and denied his father as well—effect the king's death, the king that will be, at the time I now speak of.

'And so then he, your young lord, will come at last to his own death.'

His own death. So here it is. Will it indeed have come in some way from his father, this death? How is it 'his own'? Did *he* make it so? That I could believe. There's death in his words as well. And I could believe he'll have stayed to find his death here, will not have gone away—could not take himself away.

And me, do *I* have my own death that I cannot find a path away from? Is there a death I may find that will be away from here, a death that will be my own, and not one that some other lay down for me? And what other?

'And another king will come. And that will be it.'

She took a breath.

'I wish it did not have to be so, but it does. There's no way out.'

She left.

4

There was one more time when I went with the maid over the mountain, to this hamlet where she had left that daughter she had, and this time my brother was with us. Up we go, up over the mountain, and down where he had not been before. Down, down, down, but now we face the sun.

There's a difference in the green of the grass—but that could be the sun on it. And by the path are some flowers I have not seen before. Flowers have been my love for as long as I remember, and most of them I know. It may be, I think, that the maid would know what they are, but I do not ask. I keep my thoughts in my own mind, my hand in the maid's, and I look over to the left. My brother, I see, is being good, held by the maid's other hand. She had night-things for us all over one shoulder. We are still quite little. Thus we go, each held by the maid, over the mountain.

Let me say what I know of the maid's brother, Mark. He was on his own, and he took in the maid's daughter when she left where she had been before, to come to us. There must have been some reason the maid's daughter did not come to be with us as well, but at the time I did not think of this. I took it as it was. To me, as well, the maid was all.

When she would go to see them, I think it was more to see Mark.

And you could see the joy in *his* eyes. You could see it now as we come down the path and there he is, out of doors, waving to us with his one arm, his left arm—the 'arm that was left', he would say. The other he lost as a soldier. Patient Mark. It could have rained and he would have been there, to see us come.

We go in to see the maid's daughter.

'My daughter'—this from the maid to me, as if we had not seen each other before. And worse, you would think she did not like to have to say these words.

There was, indeed, something a little harsh all the time in how the maid and that daughter would speak to each other. The effect was of two that are not at all close, and have not been so for a long time. For the maid, it may be the daughter was a memory she did not wish to remember. As for the daughter, she stayed by Mark, held him by the hand, as if to keep him there—in his own home! And I did not see this at the time, but it may be she did not like how close I was to the maid.

Well, here we are. We have come. More than before, there's something in the daughter's face I do not like, and we say nothing to one another. Still at night, when we go up to bed, we do not speak. This time we are two in the one chamber, for my brother is in the other. Indeed, we are two in the one bed. We did not speak as we unbraced each other. We did not speak in bed. She did not look at me before she turned over.

Before we had all gone to bed—it was late when we had come there—Mark had given us what it took him all day long to make for us: his 'poor fare', in his words. He was—how was this now?—I think he was steward to some lady that had lost most of what she had, but he stayed on, almost out of charity. As a steward he would know how to keep a home: he would know how to wax a table, hard with his arm as the maid did, how to lay things out.

At that table the maid is on my right, then my brother, then Mark (there to hand him things), then the maid's daughter, on my left.

And here's what we had. I give it here as he did at the time, in his own fair hand, as if we had been at the king's table—which indeed we could have been:

Dupped Dove in the fashion of Denmark

Heart of Owl, with rose honey

Beard of Cockle, cold

Heels and Ankle, jangled

Ladies' Joy, larded with rue

Sweet Tongue, on a bed of ground fennel

Puffed Paconcies

Twice-Turned Shoulder of Young Robin, in a stole of rosemary flowers

Valentine's Eyes (which I remember you have to steep in something for a long time, but I cannot remember what)

Saint's Bells, with violets

'Saint's Bells à la maid', Mark would call them, and at this the maid would look down.

'Fie!' she would say. 'Please, not again.'

I remember that night so well: Mark's joy, the glass and other things on the table (all gone now, for the lady is dead and Mark had to go from his home), the maid's 'Not again.' And as I look—as I see now more than I could see then—I see in the maid's eyes a joy like Mark's as she's turned to him, the joy of two as one, the joy of being home. She had a home with us as well. But there's a difference with us. And I think it's from this time on that I come to know what that difference is. This home, here, is more. This is truly a home.

I like most of what we have, but not the beard of cockle. I give mine to the maid. I see my brother does as well.

Then we play Coach and Tenders, and before long we have to go to bed.

'Betime, betime', goes the maid to my little brother. He still could not say it right, and we would say it as he did.

I know we are to go out again in the morning, and I fear the maid's daughter will come with us. But she does not, and, from that look she's given us, I do not believe she would wish to.

My brother rises before me and comes to the chamber where I still have my head down. The maid's daughter lay there by me, quite still. My brother does not come in the bed with us. He would know not to. I help him with his clothes—that's what he's come for—and we go out of the chamber, heels raised up as we go, whilst I look over my shoulder at the maid's daughter on the bed.

Mark is still in bed: he had had a long hard day. But the maid is up, and we all go out for the morning.

We do not know, my brother and I, where we are to go. We do not mind: the maid must know, for she treads on, face to the heavens and the morning, with one of us again in each hand.

It's cold. My eyes weep.

So we come, on the path that would redeliver us home tomorrow, to a green door in the mountain—a grass-green door we did not see the day before. Was it there?

Without knocking we go in: the door falls away at the maid's raised hand, to close again when we have all come in to this chamber.

There is no window, and all I may make out in there is the pale breath of some other being.

'This is the Lady Profound.' The words are the maid's.

'She's not a Christian, is she?' I ask. I cannot think what made me do so—as if I did not know what the Lady Profound was. Some fear it must have been.

'No, my love. She may see what cannot be seen. She may tell what no other hath powers t' tell.'

From my brother there comes nothing. We all go down, knees on the ground. We know right away, my brother and I, that this is what we have to do.

I see now in the maid's hand some violets. I see the maid give these to the Lady Profound—and indeed this is she, the one that all speak of but not so many have seen. And now, as my eyes tune in to the little that comes from some wax in a glass at the lady's right ankle, I see the Lady Profound.

What may I say? All I remember is an effect of pale green, a piteous look, an owl on one shoulder. But more than this I cannot say.

Then it comes to seem that she will speak, and she does so by means of the owl: what she would wish to say comes as the owl's speech.

It's hard to look at this owl, it's so wretched and cold, held there in a false night, day in and day out. But it's hard not to look, when what you may see is an owl with the command of speech:

'Expectancy i'-i'-is a mould o'-o'-on the ha'-ha'-

hand, and remembrance nothing. Take up the snow o'-o'-of now. Take i'-i'-it in your ha'-ha'-hand and see it go. This i'-i'-is the death of now, and this is all now i'-i'-is: now is not so long that you may say 'now'. It's o'-o'-over. Come up and see me some time.'

I see the owl's eyes now. They do not seem to know what goes on here. These words do not come from them. They look out at us as if there's no mind in there.

We say nothing, my brother and I. We each look to the maid to tell us what to do. She does not seem to be at all affrighted by the Lady Profound and the owl, but we find it hard to be quite so composed. We did what it seemed we had to do. We stayed still, knees on the ground, as if to pray. The maid answers—not to the owl but to the Lady Profound:

'We are here to know more than thy blasted moan. We have come all this way for thy counsel.'

I think the Lady Profound—the Lady Profound's owl, that is—will speak again. Then I think she—it—will not. Then I do not know. Then the words come:

'A'-a'-ask what you will a'-a'-ask. T'-t'-take what you will t'-t'-take. Know what you will know. Play it again, Sun.'

The maid rises to this, rises from the ground, and so do we:

'No more of these daisy thoughts! We have to have thy help—as thou and thy speech-master well know. These two young things I have with me, they have to have thy help—one of them most of all. Speak what thou must to them, not what thou'll like to.'

'S'-s'-speech i'-i'-is locked and cannot be blown here and there, one way and another, by the will. Not by your will and not by mine. T'-t'-take mind: you have no way to find for yourself what to say; you cannot do so. There is one that lay down your words for you. And mine. Do not blame my words, for I did not make them up. They are made for me, as i'-i'-indeed are yours for you. Truly, my sweet, I do not give a doublet.'

The maid by now is up and waving a hand as if to wish the Lady Profound would go away.

'I do not believe this.'

'Believe what you will. Think what you will. Do what you will. I'-i'-it will all come out as i'-i'-it must. Do not be deceived by hope, for hope i'-i'-is fouled stockings. You have not seen nothing ye—'

Then the maid—and I still cannot quite believe it, never mind that I was there—with a raised arm goes at the Lady Profound, and in the knocking and the shaking and the waving of the two of them, the wax falls and goes out. Now we may see nothing.

This goes on for some time. I look at my brother. I believe he took a look at me. But we cannot see each other, no more than we may see the maid and the Lady Profound and the owl, all tumbled, as we think, on the ground, where the maid and the Lady Profound have a go at each other. What will come of all this?

I do not know if the maid had been here before. I would think she was, one other time, so she would know what to do. But she did not say. And is this the way to go on with the sovereign lady of the night?

My brother and I say nothing. I bended over to him and held his hand. Hard to believe that out there it was still morning, whilst here, in the night, these two tear at one another. Now they seem to be down on the ground; now they are up again. This goes on and on.

At length they come to an end and are composed again, almost so, the maid with us and the Lady Profound where she was. Their breath is harsh-blown. I see the Lady Profound make the wax go again. We do not know quite how—no-one will say—but the one that lost was the Lady Profound. This means—we had to make this out, my brother and I, at home again—that now the Lady Profound will have to speak some more, and this time speak true.

She does so. Well, the owl does so.

'The daughter of the cold green mountain does not know which path of two she should take. Should she go to the right and do what she will? Should she go to the left and do what she must? More: is there a difference? What answers will she give? There is more than one lesson she will have to find out, you see. She cannot say which way to go whilst she may see but one, the one she is on now. She will have to come to the other. But which is that? The will, the must? Will she find out? Must she find out? What help may she hope for? Little from me. Little from you. Little, so little, from that brother she is with. There is another, another that will show the other way. Let the daughter of the cold green mountain look for him—if indeed it is a him, which it may not be. More I cannot say. More you must not ask for. More you will not ask for.'

I may not remember this speech quite as it was, but I know these words are close to it, for most of them are locked away in my memory, to take out now and again for a perusal. They are words that—as was my hope—have meant more than I could see in them at the time. As the months go by, it will come to me that there are two key things for me to keep in mind from that morning: the words, and how it was that the maid took me to see the Lady Profound. She must have had a reason. She had given me something in that night-time speech of death and the end; now she had given me something more.

As for the words, I would think more and more of the one that was to show me the way, the one that was to help me. Could it be my father, as at one time it seemed to me it must be? If so, when would his help come? And what was the reason it could not come now? If not my father, was it Gis? The king? The maid's brother? There are not so many more men I know. But then, as the Lady Profound's words left it, the one that helps could be a she.

Now I know the one it is. Now I know it must and will be one I did not know at that time, one that would be with me some day, one I did not have to look for, one that would come, one that is now here.

With that, it seemed that this counsel from the Lady Profound was over. She let a little time go by. Then the owl, to show this was the end, did speak one last time:

'What you have had from me is—', and then it goes by letters, as if this is one of the words it cannot say, 'T-A-B-O-O. Do not speak of this to another soul.'

The maid's eyes are still on the Lady Profound as she rises up: 'We will not.'

'All of you.'

So we all—and we all are up now—say these words again: 'We will not.'

'You have promised, as a soldier on his sword.'

'We have promised, as a soldier on his sword.'

'Go!'

That was it. No 'fare you well'. Nothing of that. No more gifts as we left.

Being out of the green door now, out in the sun—it blasted my eyes—we left to take the path to Mark's home again, the maid and then us two. We did not think it right to speak. Nothing more did we two say that morning. When you are little there are things you know to do, and not make an argument of it, not ask for a reason. But this time there was a reason: the maid had to think. There she was, before us, head down, eyes down. And us two, on the path, quite still, hand in hand.

Never again did we speak of this access we had had to the Lady Profound. But late that night, when we had gone up to bed and the maid held out my night-shirt for me, there was a look she had. If I close my eyes, I may see it still, that look, that hard look, as if to say: 'Remember'.

I do. And before that night is over I will see in my mind's eye so many things I do not know—one upon another, now this, now that—that it is as if there are bells all over the chamber, as if my head will be blasted by the music of them.

There are bells that sing a jangled ground and the end of another day, bells of blame and beauty, dalliance and doubt, bells of glass, blown bells, cast bells, bells shaking and knocking, bells Christian and other, bells of pastors, of Sundays, of death and remembrance, bells that keen, bells that keen for a god gone, bells of things and thoughts tumbled out of tune, bells of horrors, of a wish that was denied, of charity fouled, bells from the dead of night, bells of before and again, bells that do no more than tell the time, bells at doors, bells of givers when they could not be patient, bells of a cold morning on the mountain, bells that speak like one sword on another, bells of flowers, of columbines waving in the morning, bells of a tongue touching memory, bells to restore to us months in a day, bells on the arm of a fair lady as she rises to sing, at the ankle of a young king in a state of fear, on the sandal of a saint as she goes up to pray, bells that tell the steward when he must obey, bells that tell a daughter what she had to know.

5

To see a fair lady upon a night coach.
Stone on the right hand and bells on the heels,
She shall have music when

When indeed there still *was* music. When my brother was still a little primrose. Then I would sing to him like this, and we could go on all morning that way, when we had done with the other things we had to say to each other.

And when I speak of my brother at this time—of how he was and of how I was with him—I have to say I did good things for him, never mind what was to come. I did all that was in my powers for my brother. Remember: I was young as well. I may see now that there was more I could have done, more I could have given him—but not then. Then I left nothing out; then there was nothing that could have been done that I did not do. I did not have to think what to do: I let love show me how. And if I had it to do all over again, there would be no difference.

Still, I must take some of the blame for how things turned out with him for a time.

Young King Poll
Was a merry young soul,
And a merry young soul are you.
He did call for his grass,
And did call for his owl,
And did call for his ladies two.

With my father away for months on end, and the other

one—*she*—being as she is, it falls to me and the maid to do what we may for my brother—to give him the love and affection a young one should have.

It was right we did that. I cannot think it was not. And it was *his* right. We had to do what we could to make up for what was not there.

But I know now that we could never, alack, give him all the things he should have had from my father, not to speak of the other one. Do what we may, we cannot. And this becomes more true as the months go by. We see it.

'It was nothing you did', I say. 'Father's not himself this morning.'

'If he's not himself, then what *is* he?'

'Not himself. That's all. It's something you say.'

'I know. I remember. You tell me again and again. It's something you say.'

'Would you like to come with me up the mountain?'

'No.' He will not look at me.

'Do you have a reason?'

'No.'

'Is it what I had to say to you last night?'

'No.'

'Will you come tomorrow?'

'No.' Still his eyes are down on the ground.

'Will you come another day?'

'No.'

Tumbled, tumbled, little sun,
How I think what you have done,
Up a

But I cannot see—cannot see where it will come from, and when: this cold breath of fear. In the months when it rained, there we would be: him by himself (I would know not to go up there), and me on my own as well. I look out of the window, at how it rains, and I think. Then he'll come in and ask me, sweet as could be, to go with him to the music chamber, which they keep locked, but I have the key. I know what he's come for: all he would have to do would be come in and look at me. In the music chamber is a little table, where she let us play Go. For Go whiles away the time; Go would give us something to do other than think.

You cannot play Coach and Tenders with two, but Go you may. Indeed, for Go you have to have two and no more. That's one of the things I remember from a time I do not like to remember. You have to have two. So he had to have me.

I think my father must have seen more than he seemed to at the time. One morning he turned to us to say he would find a Go master for us, 'being as how you play Go all day long'. That was so like him: if we did something, we had to do it well. And that was how I took it at the time.

He did not let time go by. Before we know where we are, we are at the table in the music chamber, and here's this Go master to give us a lesson.

'Right. Go One-O-One.

'You must have another with you to play Go, as you know. This is not something your honourable brother may do by himself; this is not something you, honourable lady, may do without him. For each of you, there must be the other. In Go, you are locked to each other. It must be so. Locked to each other and locked away. It must be as if you two are all there is in all of time.

'You may play green, honourable lady. If not, then you, honourable youth, must play green. One of you must play green, the other the other. There is no other way.'

His right hand, there, on the table.

'You may speak as you play, but you do not have to. For Go you do not have to have words at all.' That was good, for us.

'But to go on— Ha! *Go* on!' My brother let out a sigh 'Well, to go on, you take up one of your men in your hand, like this.' And he was touching my hand. I draw it away, no more than a little, and he lets go. Ha. No more of that.

'And indeed your men may be lost that way. This is the way of Go. They come, they go.' Another sigh from my brother.

'Where was I? So, indeed. You must not let the other take them! Keep that in mind! See how here your honourable brother could take you? And he will! And if he does, you will have lost face. So you have to think.

'There is a way to make your play well, and more than one way to do it other than well. It may take you months to find a good way to play one of your men— and still there will be a better. You may never find that way. You may wax and pale and never find it. That would be wretched for you—and it will be more wretched if you come close to the way and still cannot find it, but know it is there and you cannot find it, know that you could go on and on and never find the way.

'If you are to have a better hope that you will, one day, find the way, then Go must have all of your mind. All of your mind must be Go-mind. That's all there is to it. That's all I have to say. So please: play Go and do not think of these other things. It's better that way. This is the way to—'

'Go!'

That was my brother. Like the owl of the Lady Profound's.

Cock a daisy do,
My lady's lost two shoon,
My master's lost his fennel staff
And does not know what to do.

I have my hand on his little shoulder.

'Do not do that.'

I keep my hand there.

'Do not do that, *please.*'

Still I keep my hand there.

He turned, and as he did so, my hand falls.

Rains, rains, go away:
Come again another day.

Another day, when we have gone out, he treads before me up the mountain, and does not look to see where I may be. All the way he never turned. By the time we come to the mountain's brow—where in months gone by we would play all the long morning—we are quite puffed out. We look out yonder—that way to the watchman's ha-ha, and over there to where the holy men have their home, and so on down to Twice-Way

Green. There is no sun: late that day it rained, I remember. We go down again, again with him before me.

That may have been the morning when father, as was his way, held up his hand to say we would all go away to find some sun—I cannot remember where. I wish we had done that more, for things are better with my brother and me when we are away. For what reason I do not know: I take it as it comes.

It may be there's more to be observed when one's away, so that the two of us are little observers of this and that all day long: how they make flowers in bended glass (and you have to see them as they do it); the way men will look at things before they take them, touching them all over; the holy well that you may look down and see no end; all the things they have in the baker's window; the Hope Falls (a must-see). We would go from one of these things to another, him and me, and he would tell me his thoughts—of what we had seen, and other things. It seemed he could speak truly to me again, tell me of himself as he did before. But at home it was never like that now.

There's never an argument. It's not that. It's more that we keep touching on things that we each know the other does not wish to speak of.

The Go time is long over, and if we are in the music chamber now it's indeed to play music. With music, thank God, you cannot speak. But when two of you play music, you may say things to each other you could never say in words, and that may not be so good.

Did I say before—I think I did—that my brother was better than me at music? That was all right; I would like it when I would come home to find he had gone there to play by himself, for by now he had a key of his own, and I could go in, and him not see me. But when it's the two of us, he *does* mind that I play worse, and he does *not* keep his thoughts to himself. There would be a raised shoulder, a look—most of the time with no words, so we could have given the effect, to one that did not know us and did no more than look in from the door, that all was well. It was not.

There was something by Beard we would play then: 'Boré in B'. It was hard for me, and if we had a go at it late at night—as we would, when my father, the maid and *she* had all gone to bed—I would find I was out of breath some way before the end.

'Come on!' This was him. 'And give it more affection! This *grave* means it should be noble: you take it more like death!'

I would say nothing to this. I took it as his way, no more than that. I could wish he had been more patient, and it made me fear for him: it's not good to see how your own brother becomes unkind, ungracious. But there it is: he was no saint.

Then, if we should play it over again. I would be worse than before. For him, that would be it. At something out of tune from me, it would all be over. He would be up, and then, with an oath, he would go.

It was no better when I could keep up with him, and not come in late. We would go on to the end, but all his jangled thoughts would come out in the music.

What did in Cock Robin?
'I', the owl did say,
'When you had gone away,
I did in Cock Robin.

From when was it like this? There had been that time, long before, when we did not speak at all, and when the music chamber stayed locked—when all the commerce we had was by means of brief letters. These we meant for my poor father: we would take them up to him. I have some of them with me still:

(Not all of them are well composed; we are so young at the time.)

'My brother recks it all.'

'If O goes to heaven, I would like to go to hell.'

'He will never obey me, and he must not play with my perfume. I will not have it.'

'My grace'—I think he meant 'glass'—'is my own. Tell O.'

'Keep you-know-what out of my chamber. And make him give me the sandal he stole.'

'I done not take O's violets. No how.'

'What is the purport of these letters if my brother cannot rede?'

'I do not like to go with O to the mountain.'

Rosemary pale, daisy, daisy,
Rosemary green,
When you are king, daisy, daisy,
I shall be keen.

But keen as I still would be all this time to help my brother, it comes to seem to me more and more that there's little hope. We had been almost one being. Now we are two—and two that do not know one another, never mind two that had some affection for each other, for I could not show my love now and he seemed to have lost his.

Worse was the doubt. Had we truly had what I think we did? How could that sweet little brother of my memory have turned in to this? I come to fear I know nothing of my brother and never did. And that will make me fear there's nothing of which I may say: 'This is true'. If not him, then what may I keep and know that I have? What may I close my hand over and never let it go?

Had I let *him* go when I did not have to, when I could have done something but did not? Had I let him down? If so, it would have been at the time *she* left. And now I would have to make up for it in some way: that was all I could think. As to how, nothing I did was quite right. I could see that. I could tell there was a way I could not find, words I could not say—words that would have made a difference to him. So it went on. If I could find the words now, late as it is, I believe it would still help—help him and help me. If I could say—no more than this—something of what was in my mind at the time, that could do some good. But, again and again, when I say something to him, it comes out cold and false.

It may be I should let time do what must be done: there's reason to hope it will.

As for the time of which I speak, all he will say is that now he's being himself, and, if I do not like it, I do not like him. No more than that.

'You never remember, do you? You never know what it means. I do not love you. I do not like you.'

This little bore's gone to mark it,
This little bore stayed at home.
This little bore took dupped dove,
This little bore had non,
And this little bore did weep 'O, o, o!'
All the way home.

6

When my father was away, be it for no more than a day and a night, I would receive letters from him, and these I would look at over and over again, my hand touching the words, would lay them where my brother could see (and he would let me see his), and then keep them in my closet where no-one could find them.

That was where, at one time, I would keep all the things that meant most to me: some violets given me by a young soldier, now withered but still with a little perfume to them; a Valentine from another (we had been at the watchmen's hey and had gone out to see the night); a stone; a sovereign; a glass heart from I do not remember where; a little wheel my brother had made.

The letters are there still, with all the other things, so I will take them out and look at them from time to time. But most of them I remember by heart.

'My daughter,

'All is well. My tongue is better, and so are my eyes. It all turned out to be nothing. No doubt it did me good that I stayed in bed for a day before I had to go away.

'The fashion here you would not believe! And what they give you each night! Night on night all I have had was heart!

'I have given my speech now: I did so from memory. If you like, I will give it when home with you, so you may see how well I do it. What I had to say of Honour and the State Good did, I must say, go truly well. It made the king himself say he would like to know more! I'll see him before I go.

'With all a father's love.'

He was a master of the speech. Never—of this there

may be no doubt—did he give other than a good one, and he could do so when he had to speak on something that was not at the time close to his heart.

Many of them I remember, as well as I remember his letters: the speech on Love and Affection he did for the maid and the baker, the one on What To Give To Charity for the Chamber of Commerce, the one on *Dead Souls* that's gone down so well each time with the pastors of All Saint's. But if I should redeliver them, I could not do it the way *he* did it.

If he had to give a state speech here, we would all be there. It would be a day of joy for us: me, my brother (most of the time), the maid, for as long as she was with us. Not the other one: she would never come.

He could make a speech that was quite brief, but most of the time he did not. He held you. And you would wish he would go on to morning.

When a speech by him was promised, never mind where, they would come from all over to be there, all of them with expectation in their eyes. You would see a green youth by one with a beard, a soldier by a music head, two keen observers by some beauty in a stole. They would all be quite still for as long as he would speak. Each face would show the effect he made: woe at this, joy at that. Then he would draw it all to a close, and you could almost see the words take form as he did so, and then all that were there would have to give him a good hand.

If I close my eyes, I see my father at one such time. He rises. All is still. His right arm is raised, and there is a look in his eyes as if his thoughts could still be in doubt. Then his hand falls and he's away.

It was something to remember, being at a speech of

his. The letters he would receive! 'I was there the night you made your speech on such and such.' 'Thank you for your words, thank you.' 'Here was something for me to tell my daughter one day.' 'You have such powers with words you could prove two and two make one.'

We would be there at the door to take him home when his speech was done, and they would be all over him. He had something to say to each, and would never sigh as they would go on and on with their good thoughts of him and his speech, but would look at them, with his patient eyes.

'Daughter mine,

'My tongue is, ay me, not so good. You would think I had been given something rich, but all it was—as, indeed, on each day I have been here—was more heart!

'My shoulder, as well, is not so good as it was before.

'But my eyes now are indeed better. I may see what effect I make when I give a speech. And think of this: I have to speak to His Majesty himself on Reason and Command! I'll be in ecstasy!

'I'll say more of this.

'My love to you all.'

Poor father, he was never quite well. These things with his heart and his shoulder I remember, for he would tell us of them each morning, but do so in a merry way. He's still like that. He'll come down, say what's not right with him and make little of it, and I'll say: 'Poor father!' And he'll say: 'No, no: rich, rich!' It's one of the things I love him for.

If he stayed in bed all day—as he would tell me he did

in some of these letters, and as he did at home—then in no way was that for himself: I wish it had been. No, it was to fashion his words, to think how he could redeliver some speech from before and make it better still. These are things he would have to do by himself, away from us, and where better than in bed? That was where he composed, then as now. 'That's where words come to me', he would say. 'I find them in the bed clothes.'

I wish he had been well more of the time. The end of his tongue had a little green mould on it for months, but he took it with a good grace. Another time, when he had something not right with his eyes, he could not make out letters from a table's length away. How I would wish I could take some of this on my shoulders!

'Please,' I would say, 'have this day to yourself. Give no mind to us. Go out up the mountain: that would do you good.'

And he would say, his words touching my heart: 'No, no, nothing turned in the still mind. You know how it is with me: when there's a speech to be done, I cannot keep away from it.' And then there would be all the other things he had to do.

He was hard on himself, and that cannot have been a help to his eyes, which have never been good. His left arm, as well, had little play in it.

This was all from the time when he, like so many men, was a soldier. The maid's brother Mark was in my father's command, and—this I had from Mark, not from my father, for he would say little of his youth—the two of them had been blasted by a mine as they had gone to take something up to the king's watchman. I remember Mark's words:

'It was night time, and quite still. Then all hell rained down on us from the mountain. Your father and I are out cold. We did not come to for a long time: another two had to come out to find us. Then, as we lay there, your father turned to me. He could not speak, but he did give me a look, as if to say: "Are you all right?"'

'My daughter,
'It's late now, but I had to tell you a little of my thoughts before I turned in.

'My speech before the king on Reason and Command did, I must say, go better than when I did it before. His Majesty stayed for most of it. And Lord Last—he was there as well, for as long as the king was—Lord Last had this to say: "I think your thoughts most noble, most noble", before he had to go. You must know how this would please me!

'Now I have more to do for them—a speech which I think I will call: "Should the Poor Blame the Rich?" It may be hard to make this go as it should.

'What I took for my eyes does indeed help—which is good when each day I have to make another speech!

'As for my tongue, it's better now, but my heart is not so good. There may be reason for this: the fare we had late at night this time was not heart but...tongue!

'Let me know if you receive this. I'll give it to one of Lord Last's little men, me being so well in with him now.

'Tenders to you all.'

I do not know what I would do without him.

'Daughter mine,
'I think of you and love you. I think, as well, of Little. Is he being good?

'It may be that I will not see you all for some time, and if so, there is something I would like you to tell him from me, if and when he must go away from home. This is what I would say:

' "Give your thoughts no tongue.

' "What men you know, and that show you affection, you should keep by you.

' "Give each lord your shoulder, but no madam your heart.

' "Do not take and do not give. You know what this means.

' "Look good when you go out, but doubt fashion.

' "This most of all: to your own soul be true, and it must come from this, as night from day, you may not then be false to rich, to poor."

'As to that, I think the speech I must give here may now be: "Do the Poor Shame the Rich?" I'll see.

'But please give these words to Little as they are. Speak them as I would speak them. You know how. They are noble words and should be done in a noble way. Do them from memory, if you may. Have them by heart. And keep them in your own heart.

'As for my heart, it is better, and so are my tongue, shoulder and eyes. I pray God that you are well, that all of you are well.

'There are thoughts that I have, now and then, that are hard to say to you. I would like to say more, but may not.

'With a father's love and affection.'

It was so like my father that he should give his mind most to another, as here to my brother, when he was away from home—when he had a speech to think of, when he had to look out all the time for what was being made of him by men in command, and when he had, as well, these day-to-day things with his heart, his eyes and so on.

I never had to redeliver that counsel to my brother.

As it turned out, there was nothing to keep my father from us for long. But it was good to have the words down where I could see them, and think of them, and think of how he would speak them, and so think of him when he was away. They are words to call him to mind—words he's never but been true to. He never lets himself down. And if that means he never lets himself go, it's not up to me to wish he would. But I do. There's no chamber in his heart where he is king.

'My daughter,
'Lord Last was here to see me. Think of that! And more: Lord Still was with him! Such good men. They would have stayed and stayed, I do believe, but had to be away. I think now my speech will be: "How the Poor are to Blame".

'I was up late at a show. I know you do not like the music I like; still, I think you would like this from what they did:

Love, love me do,
You know I love you,
I'll never be true,
So PLEASE, love me do.

'Well, you have to know the music. It's not at all like the king's: I'll play it for you when home—which is where I long to be!

'My tongue, heart and eyes are all well. Not so my shoulder, but never mind.

'With more of your father's love, and more to come.'

This was long before the late king died. My father was good at music, when he had the time. He would play and sing with us, and have us go over things for him before a lesson. If he could, he stayed for the lesson, and that made a difference to the lady that had come to coach us. With him there, she would find a way to make you play better. 'I think you lost the argument a little there, where it goes to another key.' 'May this be more like bells?' 'Think of this, that you have gone out in the morning to make music, and here, in the right hand, you sing as the sun rises over the mountain.' As for him, he did not have to speak.

'Daughter mine,

'His Majesty could not be there when I made my speech. But all was well.

'Lord Last and Lord Still did not come. They had given me help with it—which could well have given them their reason not to come! There was nothing in it that they did not know!

'There was a Madam Something that was there, and stayed for all my speech. And His Grace did indeed come—did I tell you of His Grace? And Lord Say and another noble lord with their daughter. I did not know that a lord could have a daughter with another lord, but there we are.

'So that was all.

'But I do not mind. Better a good speech to a poor soul than a poor speech to a good—

'No, that's not it.

'I should be in bed by now. It's late, and I'll be home with you before long. I'll tell you more then.

'May the grace of God be with you, and a father's heart's love.'

7

I think it was a little before these letters that *she*—the lady of this little home that was no home for as long as she stayed there—went.

Most of the day, by now, she lay in bed, in a chamber away from my father's. The reason was not—as with my father—so that she could do letters and things like that. No. No.

There was a time before. I know there was. I have to keep that in mind. There was a time when I could go in and out of their chamber, when the two of them had the one chamber, which was where my brother and I had come in to being. I could go in and out without fear, never think.

That's now my father's: he had stayed there when she took all she had to another chamber.

She had, in effect, left him—but not gone.

Up there she would call in men—men such as he would never receive. She was quite reckless. She had no wish at all to keep it from my father. And he could not make the lady keep it from my brother and me.

It may be that one day I'll find it piteous. But not now.

So that's how it was. I was in on it, and so was my brother. How could he not be? It was as if she had this wish to be observed. No, not observed. She had to have us know what went on, know what she was—know and have no-one to tell, so that we would have to make it seem there was nothing at all. It was a way to shame shame.

I remember young Robin, flaxen-head Robin, Robin

that was so young he had no beard, barefaced Robin. He would have seemed a sweet youth to me had it not been for what he did—and how he was. He would come knocking on the door each day at two, and I would be the one that had to let him in.

'Hey,' he would say, 'how's things?'

No time for answers. Right away he would have turned from me to go up, touching my shoulder with his hand as he went. That hand.

Then down he would come. I did not like the look on his face, the way he held himself. Quite the young courtier.

This was before the time when two of the night watchman's staff would come in the morning, and *she* would be with them most of the day. I did not know what to call them. What *she* would call them was Other and Another.

They had a key she had given them, so I did not have to see them all the time as I did Robin, which was all right by me. But I did know when they had gone up to their lady love: there was the sigh, the moan, from the door—from the bed. Then I would go up the mountain and not come down again before they had gone. And I would take my brother with me, for as long as I could make him go.

But, do what we would, we could not help but see these two now and again, here and there, for they had their home close by. And they are there still. They look at me as if nothing had gone on.

They are men—not like Robin. She had gone on to men. They have, as she would say, the bulk of men.

By now she would tell me what she did with them.

I had the call to go up there one day, before they had come. Did I know what went on? I did. Never mind, she had to tell me face to face what she was up to. And she had to tell me again from time to time, and would look me in the eyes as she did so.

'I do not know which I like more'—this was one time—'of Other and Another. You know them. Which do you like the look of?'

What did she think I could say to this?

She went on.

'Other is fair—heavenly fair from his head to his heels, all over, my Being Beauteous.'

She seemed to like to speak words like this, and know that as she did so she fouled them.

'I like it as well when he's turned away from me, when I know his fair eyes and all the other fair, fair things of him are there, but cannot see them. I know I'll see them again, all right. I know I'll see each feature of him, that he'll give himself to my perusal: he'll have to. And all the time he'll say nothing, for they know what I like, these two.

'They never speak to me, and they never speak to each other. That's the way I like it, and that's the way it will have to be.'

And I had to see all this, how she would be. I could not close my eyes.

'*I* must be the one to speak. *I* must be the one to give them the lesson they have come for—each day another lesson, each day some difference. They like it that there's this difference in what we do, and it does something for me as well, to keep them on their form.'

I still cannot quite believe she could say all this to me.

‘ “Lesson” did I say? I’ll come to that. So, they do not speak. Each of them I know to have a tongue in his head, and a sweet, sweet tongue at that. No, they have lost nothing. They have the means to speak. They have, indeed, all the means.

‘As for Another, on his face there’s more of a down-cast look. He is night to Other’s day; and where with Other you see the sun come out, with Another it’s as if it rained, and all you would wish to do now is go in, go in with him, and have your way with him whilst the rains go on.

‘Take a look at him some time. How could you not wish and hope the rains would never end?

‘With him the night comes over you: he will take you in to his night, and with his hand he will make the sun go out. There is the still of night in him. And there are the powers of night.

‘His stature is that of a god, the god of night. Indeed he is a god, made to command. But he does not. I do.’

I remember the look she had; I see these eyes as they held me. How could she do this, given what she must see in my face: a daughter’s love?

Daughter? Before long she lost all that from me.

‘He will give himself to me, and he will give me his powers of night, the powers in his arm. That arm: I have seen it shaking as he held me—shaking in ecstasy. Believe it.

‘So here they are, Other and Another, my men. As I say, I do not know which I like more. And I do not have to know, for I may have the two of them—one by one if I wish, but most of the time as they will be, here, when you have gone: the two of them with me in my chamber, on my bed, as night and day, the sun and the rains. My two men, made for me.

'And, as well, I do not know—do not have to know—which I like more out of being observed and being one of the observers. Other and Another and me: that will make two thrice over. Other and me. Another and me. And—o heaven!—Other and Another.

'Each of us may be observed and observers at the one time in what we do. This way, that way. Your way, his way. Their way, my way.

'But when it's their way—when I look at one and see in his eyes what he'll most like to do to me, have done to him—it's still my way. If I do things to please them, as I do most of the time—not all—, it's to please me as well.

'We may all be givers. We may all be given. They may give to each other, and they may give to me as they do so. I will give what I will. I will take what I will. I will keep them so that they long for what I will give and what I will take.

' "Out of your clothes!" I may say, to the two of them. If not, I may have one of them keep his clothes on—some of his clothes—for it may be better that way. I could make each of them take the other out of his clothes, and give them some music to do so. You should see it!

'It's good, as well, when you do this yourself, take them out of their clothes. They like that. And they should like what you do to them. But you should like it more.

'They'll do as I ask: there's never a doubt of that. They do all I ask.

‘ “Look at me!” “Do not look at me!” “Let’s see that again!”

‘Let’s say it’s like this: each of them will take himself out of his shirt, his long stockings (for I like them to wear stockings most of the time), and so on. I may sigh, I may moan, to please them. They know I do it for them, and do not mind. How should they mind? They are mine.

‘Then the lesson will go on. “Find another way so that he’s held where he is!” “In there!” “Not so close: I’ll tell you when!” “How steep may you make it go?” “Do you remember when you did that with it before?” “Not his, mine!” “Give it to me here, now!” I will come again another time for more.

‘But do I have to go on? The words you know as well as I do, but not, I think, what each of them means. Have no fear: that will—shall I say?—come.

‘So: Come.’ So the words indeed come, and at each she took another look at me. ‘Beauty. Tumbled. Breath. Tumbled beauty, tumbled breath. Hand. Touching. Cock. Hard. Each of them with a hard-on. Long long long. Draw. Draw in. Ecstasy. To be dupped and dupped again. To be dupped by the one and then by the other, and then by the one again, for as long as it will take that you cannot remember which is which. To have them look and look and find the doors, find all the doors. Call out. More. More. Now. To be gyved. To be jangled. To be larded. To be larded all over and in me. To be done. To be well and truly done.’

Was she done with this now? Did she think I had had all I could take? No, there would be more another day, and more again.

Did she know what she had done? She had made it so that I could not believe my own memory. I could not now believe I truly could remember: I was left in a cold night of doubt.

Some things I had that I held on to. My father, most of all—now that my brother had gone his own way and the maid had left us. My father would show me what is right and true, and what it means to be right and true in yourself.

But him, as well, she would have fouled in my mind if she could. She would tell me things that may have been true, but things I had no wish to know, and indeed no *right* to know. It was a way to show the powers she had over me.

'Your father is nothing. I know he may have had some thoughts of being made a lord, but the king, you know, does not love him, not truly. It's all for show, for the good of the state. To the king he's no more than another courtier. The king will let him go when he's done with him. That's how it is. That's how these things go.'

This is the king that was.

'There was a day, indeed, when the king held your father in some honour. But that day is long gone. It may still please them—the king and his ungracious lady—to keep your father by them, but you should see how they make a face at each other when he cannot see. Do not be deceived. We all know it: he's a bore. But they like to play with him. They love it when they make him show himself up. And then there's this, that they think he may know more than he should.

'That would be from before. Now he's nothing. His powers are over.'

The way she puffed out that 'powers': it was as if she longed to have him blown to nothing.

It was not all false. It was false in how it was meant. She would have had to know she could never have an effect on my love for my father, and could never make him seem little in my eyes. Still, she made a difference. I would look at him, my own father, with all the love I had for him, and could not say what was on my mind. And we had been so close before. We would be so again when she was gone and out of the way, but still then—still now—there are things I cannot tell him. And I see in his eyes how they seem to ask me for a reason, as they show me his love.

I could not and cannot tell him. So she is still here, one cold hand on each of us, when we speak. I could not and cannot tell him how some of the things she did would make me fear I had lost my reason—how she would then come to me at night, and speak as if she could never have been unkind to me.

'My daughter, my daughter, let me lay my hand on your brow whilst you tell me all your thoughts.'

How could I then draw away? How could I not show affection, now that she seemed to show some for me? And if by this time I could not find affection in my heart, how could I not *seem* to show it? So there I was, sucked in to a play, made to show a false face.

Not for nothing, then, did I almost wear out my mind. If *she* was like this, was that so of them all? My father? My brother? The maid? The young soldier with violets in his hand? Did they all do what they did for show, for me to see? No more than that?

But I had to keep my head. You have to tell yourself there are things you know, things no-one may take away from you. So it was with me at that time.

Still, I had to make my way from door to door, touching each with a brief hand.

I remember Sundays. I remember these wretched Sundays, when there was no lesson to take my mind away to other thoughts, and the maid had by now gone away with the baker, and my father would have to keep at it with some speech, and my brother would play music as long as I let him be (he had 'O Keep Out!' on the music chamber door, to which I had lost my key), and it was she and me.

One such day comes to mind more than most. It was late in the morning, and she and I had done what we had to: take the things from the table, see to father's clothes (this was something she would still do for him, and I would like to help). All the time she did not speak to me. Now we had nothing to do but look at one another, and as she held me with these two cold eyes, she sucked on a stone. That was all. Still she did not speak—did not *have* to speak. She sucked on a stone.

In the still of the late morning there was an expectation—and that look, that cold look, had my heart knocking. I have to do something. She will not. It's up to me. She will go on and on there, with that look held on me, and do nothing. There's nothing she'll have to do. I have lost my ground right away, my heart knocking, my hand shaking. All she will have to do is be patient.

So I tumbled out my woe. What reason could I have had to do so? This: that there was not one soul I could have turned to. My brother now was on his own path, and as it turned out, I would never again find a way to tell him my close thoughts: things went another way. My father—well, she had made it hard for me to speak to him. And the more she held me with that look, the more it seemed I had to say what was on my mind. So I tumbled out my woe to the one that had given me that woe. I had lost all hope.

I never did this again, but I wish I had not given in then. I should have had the powers of mind to face the lady out, play it quite cold. But I could not. If I had it to do over again, then I could find such powers, for there's more to me now than the poor, sweet daughter. But with that look on me, and no-one to give me a hand, I could not.

A pale stone. She took it out and held it, and turned it in the sun, so that she could look at it as I went on and on. She did so to show me how little my words meant, now that she had made me speak. But that made me go on the more. And so my shame becomes the more.

I see me there. I see me weep. I see me go on with my words, my jangled words, more and more out of breath.

O, if you could have held your tongue!

She rises whilst I still speak on, on and on. She goes out.

She was a length of hell.

I know the time will come when the glass of my memory will close over, when I will see nothing in it, know nothing, and then I must not fear but be quite still and patient, whilst my remembrances come to me again, one by one. And as my memory becomes composed again, so will I.

Mine is a memory made, as all memory is made, of what was and what should have been. Wish is close to memory, and will find a way in. Wish will not be denied. We all know that. Your memory is not one but many—a long music you have made and will make again, over and over, with some things you know and some you do not, some that are true and some you have made up, some that have stayed from long before and some that have come this morning, some that will go tomorrow and some that have long been there but you will never find them, not if you look from now to your last day, for there is no end to memory.

And memory is never still. Memory we fashion so that it will tell us what we think we wish to know. From one day to another there may be a difference in what that will be.

More than that, when you look at your memory what you see is not quite yourself, for you are more than your memory. You are all that you have been and could be. You may never, in your memory, see the true you. You are another—and many more than one. Your head is the home of difference. What does it take to see yourself as you are?

You pray for the time when you are one, when all that you are is composed to make the one you.

As for me, I know that time will come, and I will be in it and it will be in me. It may be that this is how I will know the right path when it comes: that I will then think and do, and it will be the one me that does so.

Then one day she was gone. She went in the night, and

in the morning we had a home again.

I go down before my father and my brother for some reason. I look at the things I know so well: the door, the table, the window. But they do not seem as they did before: it's as if they have something to tell me. All is still.

How do I know she's gone? I cannot remember. But I *do know*. It comes to me right away. She's gone. This is my home now. This is my father's home and my brother's home. This is home. I go up again to where they still are. Let the sun come in at my window! Let a robin sing! Before I could not truly wish for such things. Before was another day. Before is over.

I go down and lay the table.

My father did not tell us where she had gone: did he know? So in a way it was as if she had never been. We—my brother and I, that is—went on as we had. We did not think we should ask what had gone on, and I truly did not mind if I did not lay eyes on the lady again.

But that was not so for my brother, and when some time had gone by he would ask me where she could be now. I would make things up for him (it was my hope he could be turned from such thoughts, but this may not have been the way to do it), and he would make them up for himself. It was like play—but with something more to it.

'You will not see May-May again but I will,' he would say—most of all when I was in his way.

'She lost them, the eyes she had—remember how they would look at you? She went out to look for them, bended over, with a hand on the ground. She never could find them. She went on and on, day and night—for what is night to one with no eyes? And still she goes on, one hand on the ground, and the clothes she had on when she left are now all fouled. No-one will speak to such a one as she is.'

'She *does* love me. She will call me when she is here again.'

'She took up with that young soldier, but then lost him to another. She's lost all memory of us.'

'She is in heaven, with God, but will come to see me again and give me all I like.'

'She was in the chorus of a play, and now she's a lady of the night. Each day she becomes another, and each day is worse than the last.'

'She will remember me and give me a sweet when she comes, I know.'

'I know: she's the king's lady. That's it. She went to the king. She took over from the one that was there. She's with the king, and each day, almost, we see each other, and do not know it.'

8

Him—let me speak now of him: the young lord.

Now that I come to think of it, I cannot see what reason I could have had not to do this before, for he was there all the time, with my brother and me—with us each day, almost, from when he was little. It's not as if I have lost my memory of that—of him. How could I have? No, it's more that he was such a feature, being there with us, that he's never but in my thoughts as I remember. He's like the grass and the mountain.

Well no, he's not. I have to say it's not been like that with him for quite some time now. He's here still, indeed, but in a way, it's as if he's *not* here. You have turned to speak to him: you have him in your eyes, and his eyes seem to be on you—you think so—but it's as if his mind is on something quite other. He's lost to you. And it will go on like that when he comes to speak. It's as if his mind is two: one to speak, to look at you, to be with you, and one not. And it's been like this from long before the king his father died.

I know there are some that think his father's death made a difference to him, that he was all right before that. But believe me, he was not.

Still, there was a time when he was not so hard to be with: I have to remember that. And it's not that he's *hard* to be with now. It's more this, that it's not the way it was—not for me, and, no doubt, not for him. I believe that's so. All that is hard for me now—and each day becomes more so—is to know what goes on in his head.

No, again, 'hard' is not right. It's not hard. Nothing's hard with him. I love him still—as a brother, let me say—and I love being with him still.

Be that as it may, it's true that we do not have now what we had before, he and I—and my brother with us as well: the Thorny Thrice, as my little brother would call us then.

So let me go right away to that time long before this, that better time when he was young and so was I.

With a king for his father, he did not have so many they would think it right for him to play with. We had that honour—if honour it was. It could seem, at the time, more like something you did on command—to him as well, for he would tell me so.

They may not have meant to make it seem like something he had to do, but so it was. He had to wear his play-clothes. He had to have a steward to take him to us. He had to be observed all the time. Then they would take him home. That was the way of things.

If we went to where *he* was, it was worse. You could not take a breath without one of the ladies—two we had to mind us—would look up and say something. You could not go out to find saint's bells without the two of them would come with you.

One day we all went out like that, and then, at a look from him, I turned to go in again, and he went like all hell up the steep path to the mountain, and.... What did my brother do? Stayed still, that was it. That made them give us another lady to be with us all the time from then on, one each.

All this was so that he would know his difference from us, right from when he was little. They did what they could to take the joy away. And we—we had to find what joy we could, find what we could say and could not say, with their eyes on us.

That made us the more close. It was us and them.

It was that way all the long months of his youth and mine, the months when the sun stayed where it was, and it would seem in the morning that the day would never end. He would come, with his wretched steward and the ladies. Most of the time it was for the day, but now and again he stayed over, and the steward would be in my brother's chamber, whilst the ladies went home for the night. As for us, we would all be in my bed (for they would let us do that, being all so little at the time), and we would speak of this and that. If not, we would be quite still and look out of the window as the day went. Many a time I turned to him, to see his eyes.

What I could *not* see then, but remember now, is that he would seem to find with us something he could not find at home.

No, that's not quite true. He did not *find* it, not with us. But with us he could *look*.

Now, as I think of that time, one memory falls over another, and what's left to me are remembrances all gyved and jangled. I have to keep one from another, keep now from then. I have to keep to the time we had before he would, little by little, close himself up to me—and, it may be, to himself. I have to think of that time before he went away from me, little by little, like the end of the day.

Do I have to say that he had, when he was at his own

home, all he could wish for? That was all well and good, but it would have been better if I could have been there more of the time. If I was not, and my brother was not, he had no-one to speak with, play with, be with. All he had was things. And I think he would come to think of himself as one of these things. He was left more and more out of tune with himself.

This is not something that time will help. No, it becomes worse and worse. And it did so. I could see that. Young as I was, I would ask him what I could do to help, when he was with us but seemed out of it—as many a day he did. But he could not tell me.

If I say he would seem 'not himself', that's not quite right. Before long, being 'not himself' was how he was. There was no ground to him. And I had to take him as he was—if still hope that one day he would find some other that could help him.

It was not that he lost his love for his father, not at all. That love was unmatched, and was more, I think, than his father's love for him. If he still rains love on his father now, with his father gone, so he did then. And from his father love rained so little. His father was not unkind, not that. But the late king did not know how to be a father—did not know that one had to be a father, that this was something one had to *do*. The king was the king. What should the king be more? To us, my brother and I, the king could show some affection, a little. But not to him.

I see him now, the king as was, in my mind's eye. Must I remember? It's hard to think it's been no more than two months, two little months.

When I was at the grave that cold morning—with my father and my brother, all of us as one, which by then was not the way of it most of the time—I had columbines in my hand. We could not sing (we did not know there would never be music again); we could not weep.

He had to be at the other end from us, by himself, his clothes done up to keep out the rains, his eyes down on the violets in *his* hand. We all had flowers that day.

The day before, when his father had died, he had come right away to be with us—this time it was *not* something they made him do—and he had stayed the night, as long before. Now he could have his own bed, which had been the maid's.

One night was all it was. Then his time with us was over—for good, it seemed. We did not know if he would have things to do for the state. As it turned out, he did not. But he did have to be on hand.

And now here he was, at the other end of the grave. And *he* could not weep.

As we left, some of the ladies turned to one another to say they could not make him out. What reason could he have not to weep, given his love for his father? Was it that he did not wish to make a show? Was it that he held himself in, did not let go, so that he could do what he had to do?

He observed all there was to be observed. He would look at me from time to time, as we all turned to the grave to pray. There was nothing in his eyes.

I go again to what he was like when he was little.

When he would come to play, the maid would take

us all up the mountain, and then at length we would come down again, with the sun. And his steward would be a little way away. (No ladies: this was before we had to have them with us as well.) For that steward it must have been such a bore. But we had no thoughts for the steward.

If it rained we stayed in. That he seemed to like more, and as for us, we did not mind. The maid would tell us things by heart, of the Snow King, the Lady and the Rose, the Green Men, and such. And he would love this. He would be quite still and composed, in his play-shirt. I would look at him, and it seemed that the words meant more to him than they did to us, to me. It seemed as if I could see what they meant to him from the look in his eyes, from how he held himself. It was almost as if I could keep up with the words that way, and close my mind to the maid. I would look at him as he sucked up the words and what was in them, and it would please me that we could do this for him: there was so little we could.

This was all—I do not have to say—long before he went away to be a scholar. This was when there was nothing to keep him from us. If we did not see him one day, we would know they would have him with us tomorrow. Tomorrow we would be with one another again.

But by the time he went away it was not like it had been. He would still come. But he would speak as little as he could, and think before he did so. Two words from him was a speech. There had been a time when he was as close to me as my own heart. Now he was not. Now he held me at arm's length. No. It was something other than him, something that held him as well as me, the two of us at arm's length from each other.

I do not know what it was, but he had gone from me. He would go more. He was a youth now, and not a youth you could know well.

Then again, I could see now that I never *did* know him, not truly know him. The young do not know the young. But they see and they remember. A little of what he had been was in him still, for me. That little I held on to. And he was still in my thoughts all the time. He is so now, more than most.

But when I think of him, I think of all I do not know. For some time now he's given away so little of himself that I would have to say 'I think him' more than 'I know him'. I have him in my thoughts—and in my memory.

I wish he could know that. I wish I could tell him. I wish I could find the words to tell him. But I cannot. In these last months I have seen him more again. He'll come to me and ask me, his eyes locked on me as he does so, to think of him—not pray for him, but think of him, think *with* him—and to tell him that I do so, and that I will do so, for as long as it will take. Each time I have promised. Each time I tell him I *do* think of him, all the time; he does not have to ask. And he will cast his eyes away from me and go.

Another time he'll come to me and do no more than look at me, his eyes hard on mine. One day, when he was like this, I had to say something. Did he think I was the one with the answers? Did he think I, like them, would keep things from him, make him believe things are other than they are? Before I had done I could see this was not the way to go on. Now I know what to do: keep still, no words.

There's something he must have from me, and he cannot tell me what it is. If he could tell me, I would give it. But it may be that to tell me would be to have it lost. That would be the end. So by the look on his face he'll ask and ask and ask—for more each time, it will seem. And I know that nothing I could say would be right.

There was a time when I would hope that one day I could know what to say—could come up with it, and all this would be over. But that hope's gone. I do not know—and I know I'll never know—what it is he must have from me. I do not have that access to his mind I did have; I cannot be in there with him. All I may do is have him here in mine.

I have him here now, from another day long gone, when he had come to be with us for some time. My brother was away with Gis, which meant he could take over my brother's bed, and they did not think he had to have a steward with him now, and we had lost the ladies for good, and my father was most of the time in bed with some speech. She? She had gone, not so long before. So it was we two. And still at this time there was nothing he had to keep from me. We could truly be as one.

We would be up with the sun each morning. We had no lesson to keep us in, and so we would go over the mountain to see the holy men and play the bells, then take the path to Long Wheel, where there's what's left of a grave-ground from before the Christian time, then come home again.

All day long we would speak—and again at night, and almost to morning, with me in my bed and him over there, his shoulders upon the door of the closet—and speak of many things: of memory and how it is that we remember, of if there is an end to reason and if that is where you find God (this was all at a time when we would think of such things), of some poll the state took (and he would be shaking his head), of being and non-being, of words and things, of his state of doubt.

We could still, then, speak from the heart. The words would go on and on as if we did not have to think what to say.

Now it's not like that at all. Now I'll say something, and I'll look at him, and he'll have his head down, his hand over his eyes. If not that, then he'll go on with some argument, on and on, whilst I'll be left with nothing to say, and indeed there'll be nothing to say, for in the end, in all these words, he'll keep his own counsel. It'll be as if the words had not been his—as if it had all been in play, but with no joy to it. He'll be a speech without a face. And how may I speak to that?

When he's gone I'll think what it all meant. It could be there was something he would like to say—something he almost *had* to say, and would come close to, something that was right at the end of his tongue, but then he held it in. The steward was gone: he was now—this is how it's come to seem to me—his own watchman. He observed himself.

He's done this for a good long time—observed himself and observed the one he's with, to see what effect he'll have. We all do this when we are young, but with him it's gone on. And they have not seen it.

But *I* have. And I see it now, more and more. Does he fear he could give himself away? With me? If so, he does not know me at all. And if *that's* so, I indeed do not know him.

I cannot find the key to him. There was a time when I would look for it. Then I did not look.

That made no difference to him. He's not lost this wish to have me with him all the time, as if all is still as it was. But he'll have nothing to say to me, no more than this play of words. I do not mind that we speak so little of me, for that's something I never did hope for. All I wish is that it could be other than it is. I wish he could have more joy in himself: that would be something. It is not to be.

What he *will* say, now and again, is that there's no other he may be himself with. But that's not true. Most of what's himself is locked away from me, and it's been that way for a long time. It could be that it's locked away from him, as well. Does he still know what it means: to be himself?

But it means something to my father that I'll be there when he comes, that I'll have stayed with him for as long as he'll wish, that I'll never have something better to do. Of that I have no doubt: you see it in my father's eyes.

When he comes to the door, my father will go to let him in, and then close the door and look at him, as if to say: 'At last!' Never mind if we have seen him the day before, and the day before that.

Did they ask my father to do this for them? Did he take it on himself? That would be so like him: to see something that *had* to be done, and to do it—to give himself, and his daughter, over to their wish. No, not to their wish, but to what had to be done for them, and they did not know it, could not see it. That being so, they would never thank him. And for my father it would be better that way.

So that'll give me something, that I may please my father in that I please him—if please him is what I do. If I have long given up hope that one day I would come to know him, still more have I lost all expectation of something from him. That I know I'll never receive. Now he's a way to please my father. That's most of it. He's a way to give my father joy when so little will. And how could I have denied my father?

Up to the time the king died we would play music—the bells, as before, but other things as well, at home. (My brother by now had his own music he was in to, and had gone from the music chamber, given me the key.) He would love to have me sing to him, and for that reason I would love to do so. Now I may do no more than say the words, the words he would ask me to sing.

The bonny soldier now is dead,
Violets he bore me.
I will cast them on my bed,
Let it in his grave be.

But this is something from another time. Without music it means nothing. Without music it could make me fear.

There are other young men here I could be with. There was a time when two from over the way would come to ask me out with them and another 'young lady': that's how they would speak. But I could not go. What if he should come and find me gone? How could I have a good time with them like that? Now they have given me up.

So there are things I have lost, things I could have had but did not, which is all right, being as it's all for my father. But I have to say it does not make me like *him* more.

I love him. I cannot but love him. Love is not like.

It's been hard, indeed hard, to keep it up, day upon day. Without my father to think of I would not have done so.

As for him, what was his reason? What could be the end of it all? Still, he would come in the morning—never mind if we had been up late the night before—and I could not say no to him.

To speak truly, it's not all for my father. There's been the hope as well, right up to now, that I could do more for *him*, that there would come the day when we could speak to each other as we did when young—no, speak as we had never done before. And that hope's still not quite left me.

It almost went one day, not long before the king's death, when we had gone up the mountain. There was something I had to ask him: I could not go on with these thoughts and say nothing. So I did ask. It was to do with love, true love. It had to do with me and another. But it was as if I had importuned him: he turned to me with such a look in his eyes that I did not know what to do. Did I say something I should not have? What had I done? What had I lost? It seemed to me, there and then, that now we could never be close again as we had been, that now he could never show himself. It was all over. And I was to blame. We went down.

For some months I had no wish to be with him, and no wish to be without him. He had made me without wish.

I was cold. I could not speak to him. Then I could—but of other things. And before I could quite know it, my heart bore again the wish and the hope.

As for him, I see him now as one that does not have that wish and that hope—does not know what wish and hope are. They took these things from him, a little at a time. And how could I restore them? I could not.

He goes on. But there's no path that he's on. He goes this way and that.

This will make him seem cold—and he is, indeed, that: out in the cold. But, take him for all in all, he's cold without the wish to be so. He's without wish. He's without will.

All we could make, over time, was a way of being with each other. It's little help to us, I know. I do not like it. He does not like it. But it's what we have.

I have turned these things over in my mind, again and again, as if that would make a difference—as if I could see my remembrances another way, see that things have all the time been other than I think. But they have not.

There are some, I know, that think they know him better than I do, and it may be they do. But I doubt it. And then there are some that come to me as if I should be the one to tell them what they wish to know. 'Does he think it'll be better for the state if the mark falls?', they'll say. 'What clothes should I wear?' 'How's he on fennel?' 'Do you think he would like a Bells?' 'Will he give more to charity when he's king?' 'Is a little perfume all right, given that it'll be morning?' 'Does he have a death wish?' Not to speak of my brother, with his: 'What's he like in bed?'

How could they think I know? I look at them. No, they will have no joy from me. They go away and say there's no hope for me, my tongue is not my own. If not that, they make up things. Well, let them. I cannot tell another what's so tumbled in my own mind.

I cannot say—as little as this—what he's like to one that's not seen him. Are his eyes green? It may be they are; I cannot remember. And it's not that there's nothing in his countenance you would have lost your head over, not at all. Many have done: men as well. Some still do.

That's up to them. He never had such an effect on me, being as close to me as a brother when he was little. And it's not true that my father had the hope he *would*: my father would never wish for you what you did not and could not wish for yourself.

It may not have been so with the king as was. And I think the king's lady may still have such thoughts. But if so, she will have to think again. How should I be wed to one I know I cannot know? There never was a hope of that with him and me, and there never will be. That's all I have to say on that one.

Some think they know better: my brother for one,

as well as other young men that may have been deceived. I know my brother loosed his tongue here and there. But let them have their way. What they have to say means nothing to me, being such a long way from what's true. I have denied it. Still they go on. So what?

I go on with my thoughts—and it may be I think more than I should. There was a time when my father would say that to me, and say that no good would come of it. But my father could not have meant that. It was my father that *made* us think, my brother and me. That was something my father did make us do. I cannot now say: 'Let me not think'.

And indeed, as I now think, there are some things I may say of him and not doubt right away if it's so. Here's one: how he'll love it when we go to a play, and love it still more to be *in* a play. Make-believe is his one true joy.

I remember by heart one play we did, and I'll come to that. As for what it's like to be with him at a play, I have to say this: it's hard to make him keep still. He'll see himself in the play—as a lord that's given away all he had, a young soldier-king with his sword raised, one that's made an oath in expectation of imports he does not receive, one so in love with a lord's daughter that he bore on his shoulders what the father would ask. He'll be there, in the play. He'll call out; he'll weep. And all for nothing: for a play. One cannot but think: what would he do had he good reason?

I wish he would not do this, and I ask him not to, but it'll make no difference. It's something more than him. It'll almost make me fear, to see him like this, how a play will take him over.

Most of the time that's how it is, but now and again he'll be left cold by a play, and that's worse, for then he'll have to tell me his thoughts and ask me mine. In that way we almost make *another* play, a play upon the play. And as my answers are never right for him, he'll have to say more, ask me more, tell me more what I should think. There's no end to it, for when the play's come to an end, then this other play, of him and me, will go on, and we'll still be in *that* play by the time we have come home.

There may be more to this. It may be that the play truly never does end, that it goes on and on. He'll play himself, and what must I play? Himself as well. He'll take me over, as one in a play took him. He would play upon me. I have to show him what he is. Without me—indeed, without all of us—he's nothing. And we—we are nothing but him. In this play of his we all have to be him. He may see nothing but himself, as if each of us is a glass to him. That it should come to this! This is his hell, and we are with him there.

9

I come, as promised, to a play we all did—him, my brother, my father and me, we being all the cast. Like him, I love being in a play, most of all for the months before you do it, when you have to remember your words, speak them over and over with each other, find more and more what the play means. The play is not still: it becomes something. Then comes the time when you have your clothes for the show, and you all look at one another, and see each other another way. There's a difference, as well, in how you see yourself. You have lost yourself, to find yourself again in the play.

Before that, when you still do not know the words by heart, it's better to be at a table, all of you. Then you may think of how you should say the words, and of no more than that—not of where you should be and what you should do. If these other things come up, you may make a mark in long hand.

My brother would take it on himself to be the one to tell us what to do, and on this one day I well remember he was there at the table, with the play in his hand, from which he did not look up to see my father and me come in.

MY BROTHER: Good to see you.

Which he could not—but which he had to say to show how little he meant it.

MY FATHER/ME: Good to see *you*.
MY BROTHER: Could you give me a hand and be here when I ask? Thank you.

He still had his eyes on the play, not on us.

MY FATHER: Better late than never!

At this he did at last look up.

MY BROTHER: *I* would like it more if you could be here when I say. So would you keep that in mind from now on? As you may see, *he's* here.

As indeed *he* was. He had raised himself from the table as we had come in, and we had cast a look at one another whilst my brother stayed with his head in the play.

If he may be here by one, so may you.

He was waving a hand now to show where we should be: me on his left, my father at the end of the table.

ME: Hey ho, here we go again....

He went on.

MY BROTHER: Now that you *are* all here, let's give this a go. Father mine, would you do Denmark for now? Thank you. You all know where you are? So: on with it!

MY FATHER: *Did you call, madam?*

MY BROTHER: No. Could you, may be, give it some more...—so's we could, like, believe in you a little? Thank you.

MY FATHER: *Did you call, madam?*

MY BROTHER: More!

MY FATHER: *Did you call, madam?*

MY BROTHER: That's not it, but go on.

ME: *Thank you, Denmark. Would you be so good as to take the young master's hat up to him?*

I cannot remember now what this play was. We had done *All's Well That End's Well* before this, and what a night that had been—you would not believe!—on the mountain as the sun went down.

MY FATHER: *Indeed, madam.*

ME: *By the way, Denmark, this is his lordship's hat, is it not?*

MY FATHER: *I believe so, Your Grace.*

ME: *Thank you, Denmark, that will be all.*

I was the young lord's lady in this play. (Well, that's the way it goes: I could have had to make love to my brother, which would have been worse.) And he's a help. He's a reckless way with him when you are all in a play—quite a difference from how he is as himself.

MY FATHER: *Indeed, Your Grace.*

MY BROTHER: May he say this as if he means it, do you think?

MY FATHER: *Indeed, Your Grace.*

MY BROTHER: So go on then: do it.

MY FATHER: That *was* it: 'Indeed, Your Grace'.

MY BROTHER: Never mind. Go on, 'Your Grace'.

HIM: *There, Rose, what did I tell you? Denmark is in on this.*

MY BROTHER: Well done: good affection on the 'Rose'. Thank you. Now you again, O.

ME: *In on what, Do-Do?*

MY BROTHER: No, not 'do, do'. It's 'Do-Do'—you know: 'Dead as a Do-Do'.

ME: Right you are. *In on what,* Do-Do?

The young lord did not seem to know he should come in here.

MY BROTHER: Go on, there's a love.

HIM: *In on how To-To must have deceived the baker's daughter, that's all!*

ME: *I cannot think, Do-Do, that To-To would have Denmark know of his—. O, there you are, To-To. Did Denmark find you with your hat?*

MY BROTHER: *Indeed. That was what made me come here.*

ME: *My true, true To-To. You know my way.*

MY BROTHER: I may not like it, but I do know it.

ME: Hey, that's not in the play!

MY BROTHER: I know. Go on.

MY FATHER: I do not know at all where we are now.

MY BROTHER: You are not on. Remember? O: 'Now I must go—'

ME: *Now I must go and have a little heart to heart with Joy.*

HIM: *When you fair things have something you must tell one another heart to heart, what you will speak of will be men!*

ME: *To speak thus, Do-Do, becomes you not at all. Mark me, to be merry you would have to be profound.* When do I come on again?

MY BROTHER: If that means may you go now, no.

HIM: *Fare you well, my love. But To-To, tell me, what is all this with Grace?*

MY BROTHER: I think there should be more here, you know? Would he come out with it like that?

ME: No way! What do *you* think, father?

MY FATHER: Indeed, madam.

MY BROTHER: Thank you, O. It may be I'll have to give him some more here. Another speech? I'll think.

ME: It's your call.

MY BROTHER: But let's go on with it for now. *Grace? I know no Grace. Would that I could! I know I would have to love one I could call 'Grace'.*

MY FATHER: *Lord Rich is here, Your Grace.*

HIM: *O, show him in, Denmark, show him in, there's a good—*

MY FATHER: *Do-Do! I say!*

I remember how the play went when we did it: so well. My father stole the show as Lord Rich. He did it all with his eyes: the look of expectation, then of doubt when Do-Do would not tell him what he had come for. All of that he had right away.

HIM: *Be-Be! My, my!*

MY FATHER: *You see? I turned up on time!*

HIM: *So it would seem!*

MY BROTHER: *For what?*

MY FATHER: *To find you here, To-To—and good it is to see you!*

MY BROTHER: *And you, my lord. How goes it with you, may I ask?*

MY FATHER: *So so, To-to, so so. But I know you fare bet-*

ter, is that not so?

MY BROTHER: *You may say so, my lord. There are some as do not.*

MY FATHER: *Ecstasy, ecstasy! But do please call me 'Be-Be'.*

HIM: *We may let form go here, I should hope!*

MY BROTHER: *So we may, father. Thank you, Be—*

ME: *Be-Be! I do wish Denmark would tell me when you are here! I had to see to the pansies with Joy, but I do not like to be denied you!*

MY FATHER: *The lady of the May, as we know and love!*

ME: *Be-Be, sweet! Did To-To tell you Bonny and Noble did indeed take him on? As of now what he will make there is quite little, but he should do well in time to come.*

MY FATHER: *If he does not find a lady of means!*

ME: *The young do not wed, Be-Be. They have left it to us, to wed twice.*

MY BROTHER: *May-May!*

ME: Does he say 'May-May'?

MY BROTHER: He does now. Do you mind?

ME: I do, but go on.

MY BROTHER: *For shame!*

ME: *There is no shame, To-To, when one does well in imports: charity, I believe, should end at home. But let me look at you, To-To. I must say I like that shirt you have on. Where did it come from?*

MY BROTHER: *My brother.*

ME: *So like him. Young men should believe in nothing but the clothes they wear.*

My brother did To-To in his own shirt.

HIM: *I fear there may be something other than*

fashion for young men to believe in, my sweet.

ME: *Indeed? And what would that be, Do-Do?*

HIM: *Love.*

MY FATHER: *Do-Do, you speak like a green youth! Madam, I blame this on you! What did you do to make such a being in your own home?*

ME: *I cannot now remember, Be-Be. I keep Denmark as my memory and my daughter to tell me my mind.*

MY FATHER: *Indeed, that is what a daughter is for.* Did we cast the daughter?

MY BROTHER: No, but I will. Go on.

MY FATHER: *But tell me, how is Go-Go?*

ME: *My brother's daughter? I wish I did not have to remember: wed to a scholar—I ask you! One of these young men that know more words than God but will say nothing when they are at your table.*

MY FATHER: *Poor show. Not like Do-Do here.*

HIM: *I may speak of nothing, but I do so to good effect.*

MY BROTHER: I think I should be the one to say that.

ME: Well, you are not.

MY BROTHER: I'll see to that, if you do not mind. But let's go on as it is for now.

MY FATHER: *Now, To-To!*

MY BROTHER: Could you *not* come in before you should?

MY FATHER: But I was—

MY BROTHER: *Father!*

MY FATHER: *Now, To-To!*

MY BROTHER: *I know: 'Honour thy father that he may remember you in his will.'*

MY FATHER: *Indeed. But keep this in mind as well, To-To: never mind what your father may say, you should keep 'love' as the last of the words you speak, for as to effect, we may never know what effect that, of all words, will have!*

HIM: *Be-Be, you speak truly—and indeed, one such effect is what we meant to speak of when you—*

ME: *My sweet, I doubt that Be-Be will have come here so that we may tell him such things—not, most of all, before Denmark. Denmark!*

MY FATHER: *Madam.*

ME: *Pray see if there is some fennel we could have.*

MY FATHER: *I shall do so, madam. What a find you have there!*

ME: No father, that's Be-Be.

MY BROTHER: He *is* Be-Be as well as Denmark, remember?

ME: Indeed. Right. *The letters had nothing to do with it!*

MY BROTHER: What?

ME: O, I turned over before I should.

MY BROTHER: I give up!

ME: *To-To! Now that I look at you again, what means this state of your heels?*

MY BROTHER: *I lost another one, May-May.*

ME: Do you *have* to go on like this?

MY BROTHER: *I lost another one, May-May.*

ME: *To have lost one sandal, To-To, may look piteous. To have lost the two will seem like dalliance.*

10

Then there would be the morning when I had to go up the mountain and take no-one with me, up to the brow where all is green and you seem to be at the door to the heavens. That's where I go to pray, when I *do* pray, in my own words, to the God I know to have gone from us—but still I pray.

O God, what was your reason? How may I pray to you now that you have left us? You made us and you stayed, and it must have been good to know that you would be there, and would keep an eye, like a sun in the heavens, to make it day all the time. Now there is no eye on us, and the night goes on without end.

O Lord, you have gone; And are with us no more.
This is not what you promised, to the one that went up to see you on the mountain; He that held in his hand the things of your command you should not have deceived.
We had come to think you would last to the time when there was time no more; We had come to believe that you, like no other being, held in yourself the powers to be.
But you left like an owl in the night; O God, when you went, we could see no mark in the grass.
How without you could it be that the sun rises; How could each herb go on being green?
How was the sweet rose to give his perfume again; And the thorny rose to keep his beauty?

If God is no more with us, I pray to what is, be it so little. I pray to the rose as I do to the morning; I pray to memory and the wheel of time. And I pray to the day when God was; and I pray to the nothing where God was. That nothing: I cannot keep it in my mind. If I do so, it becomes something. It goes away. O nothing, you are so like God, for you, as well, have gone from us.

There was another come from God to say: God is dead.

O Father that is not in heaven, is heaven still there? Does mercy have a home? And is there ground for hope? Are charity and honour now no more than words? Is there still, to close over us, the heart of love?

11

My brother, by now, I had to think of as one of the men: he had a little beard. That made quite a difference to how we would be with one another. Each morning now he stayed in bed late—if, that is, he had come home at all the night before. And I would never see him before he was up and in his clothes: that time we had had, morning upon morning, to tell each other things was all over. Then he would go out—most of the time with two other young things. He would not tell us where they went, what they did.

One of them would come to call for him: I would know it was one of them from the hard knocking, twice.

'I'll go', my brother would say.

'Yield!', the one at the door would say. It could be more like ' 'ild', if not 'dild'.

'I do so!'—this from my brother. And then from the two of them: 'One for all and all for one!' I believe there was some way they had of hand-shaking now, but they would not let us see. What it all meant my brother never did say—not that we would ask. It seemed to be more for us than for them: a way to keep us locked out from what they did.

Then they would go, still with nothing to say to us. My father would look up as my brother went to the door, then, when the two of them had left, go on as before.

That's how my brother was. My father would keep out of his way—indeed, they did not speak to each other if he, my brother, could help it. That was one reason my father had such joy in his eyes when he was in a play with my brother, for then my brother would *have* to speak to him, which was better than nothing.

As for my brother and me, we would speak to each other from time to time, but there was something a little false in how we did so. It may be it would have been better if we could have been a little more unkind, a little more ungracious with each other, as we had before. Now I would look at him, but he could not look at me. If my eyes would come upon his, he would look away.

I remember the mark this made on me one day, with all of us still at the table, late in the morning: my brother, my father and I. We have another maid now, but she's not there: she's made something for us and left for the day.

My father rises from the table and goes, for he would know that my brother will not speak—if the young cockle should wish to speak at all—whilst he's there. That's how it is. Never does my father ask me what my brother had to say, never. Never does he ask for answers from my brother. He's left my brother to me; he'll take what comes for a time, and hope for more.

On many a morning what my brother had to say would be nothing at all: how it had rained in the night, what did I think of his hat. But there would be something more as well. In all he would speak, something other was meant. And I know where this had come from.

There had been a time, long before, when we did such two-time speech in play.

'Let's play Quoth.'

'My go then. You tell me what I have to say and how I have to say it.'

'Say "Come what may" so that it means "Death to you that denied a soldier's honour!" '

'Come what may!'

'Ha ha! My go.'

But now it seemed we did this all the time.

As for that morning, my father had been gone for as long as it took my brother to find his grass. Then he turned to look at me.

'That fashion does nothing for your bulk, you know.' And he took his eyes away. He took another draw, and again turned to me, with something harsh in his look.

'What would you like me to say?'

'Say what you will.'

'No, you tell me. I have no will.'

'Right, I'll ask this, again. Where did you go last night?'

'Out.'

'With?'

'What do you think? The Violets.' That's what they would call each other. I should have left it at that, but I went on.

'What did you do?' And here, all at one go, he loosed his hand from the table and bore his face right down at mine. His hope, I think, was to give me a look that could have withered the soul.

'Death! Death! Death!'

What should I have done now? I believe I made him think it was hard for me to keep composed, as in a way it was. I stayed where I was, my eyes on his. He had on the pale make-up they would all wear, these 'Violets', and the grass was on his breath. He stayed with his face close to mine for as long as it would take me to say twice over: 'Remember he's your brother.' And still I did nothing but keep my eyes on his. Then there was a hand on my right shoulder, as if to say this was all over now, and he took himself away. I turned to see the door close.

It did not go on for long like that, with him out each night. But it seemed long at the time. Then one day there was no more knocking, no more words at the door, no more hand-shaking we could not see, no more not being in bed before two in the morning if then, no more pale make-up and no more Violets. Now my brother would speak to my father again, and my father would ask me—I remember twice when he did so—what I had done to restore 'Little' to him (by now it may not have been a help to call him that). I had to say I had done nothing, which was true. But I doubt my father could quite believe it: he would look at me with 'I know there's more to this' in his eyes, and then speak of other things. He had my brother again: his head and his hand if not his heart. He did not have to know the reason.

What I could never say to my father—could say to no-one—was that there was a reason for how my brother now was, and that the reason was love. If he could but look, my father would see it. Young 'Little' bore himself better. Clothes meant more to him, and before he went out for the night (which he still did, but not so late) he would take a brief look at himself in the glass by the door, to see the effect he made. Then he would sing as he left—not the harsh music of the Violets, music no-one could sing, but something sweet and touching from my father's day. You could see how my father would like that.

We still did not know where he went. And I never did find out which young madam it was (there are not so many it could have been) that had given my brother a shoulder on which to lay that head of his—that head he had lost. But whilst I would never think to ask, he did let me in on his joy in a way.

Letters would come for him each morning, and some of them—not all—he would let me see. But he would say nothing, and I was to say nothing. I did not know the hand, but I do remember some of these letters well, for the lady had a way with words.

What's mine is yours and what is yours is mine,
But should I give you what was mine before?
The sweet remembrance of a libertine
Becomes, if one would tell it, quite a bore.
Let me not say, then, how some soldier's hand
Would find each night a touching way to please,
How this could make it last all morning and
That redeliver keen upon his knees.
One I remember comes to me in bed
And comes again twice more before he goes.
There was a scholar: how I held his head!
And how he sucked the perfume from my rose!
You now, and then I'll take another he,
For difference means more than length to me.

Now that my father could speak to my brother again, they could be seen with each other all over: on the green, by the falls, up the mountain, one of them with a speech of my father's in his hand. I think my father did not know quite what to make of it, and had no wish to ask.

It was a joy to me to see them with each other. I did not mind at all if this meant I was left out a little. And each of them would still wish to be with me from time to time. Never (so I believe) did my father see my brother's love letters, and never would my brother come to know what my father now and again would say to me—things to do with the state of his soul, for there was a memory he would go over again and again, tell me again and again, of how he had deceived the king-as-was so as to receive something promised by the king-as-would-be.

And there was another reason I did not mind if I was a little away from my father and my brother at this time, for I had—I may say this now—a love of my own. I did not speak of that to my brother. He had other things on his mind.

I cannot tell what you and other men
Have done before to give me such a lay
And make me think then's now and now is then:
You did as they—you took my breath away.
My powers of speech went when you took my breath;
My tongue had other things to do than tell.
You give me love and in this give me death:
I cannot say but sigh—I hope sigh well.
My mind is down. My mind is blown, o'erthrown.
Then letters form again: they come from you,
As we make love and make words that we own,
To say all we may say in what we do.
The sun is gone. Come to me now. It's late.
The love that cannot speak by love we state.

My brother had one of his letters in his hand one

morning—down at the table, with my father still in bed with a speech—when he turned to speak to me.

'Do you think I do as I like?'

'Which means...?'

'Is it indeed *I* that does things? Do *I* tell me where to go, when to go in, when to go out? Is there not another I, one I do not know, but that is in me, and it will have me do things? I do not know if I may, here and now, tell you what I will with my own mind, the mind I know.'

'You may and you are. This is what "you" are: you are what you do and what you say, and you are all you do and all you say. There's no other in there with you—but indeed, you may have an argument with yourself.'

'How if it's like this, that what you are—what was you up to now, the you that you know—is not what you long to be?'

I did not know quite what to say.

'It may seem like that, indeed it may. There are, let us say, things that are given us, that are some of what we are. They may be hard for us to keep down, so that we may do as we wish.'

'And where could they come from, these things?'

'Look up there out of the window. You see? The way you raised an arm over your eyes when you had to look at the sun: that comes from father, you know. I do it as well, now and again.'

'So there are things I do that are *not* mine, and that's one of them, as it is for you. I *have* to do it. It goes on in my head and I do not know it's there. It's not me.'

'O but it is! There are indeed things in yourself that you do not now know. In time you will find these things and make them yours. If not, you will cast them away. They may come again, but you will know what to do. The "you" that you make, day by day, becomes more rich and more in command. Some things, no doubt, are hard to master, and with these you will have to find a way to draw them in to yourself, so that they cannot take you over.'

'What if you long for them to take you, long to have no more say? What if all you are is in this state? What then?'

It is not night when I do see your face,
For with it comes the cock of morning's call:
The cock of ecstasy and cock of grace,
The cock of heaven and hell, the cock of all,
The cock that made me love and made me fear,
The cock of joy that could not be denied,
The cock to tell me what 'tis to be here,
The cock I would wish with me as I died.
Touching that cock my tongue a way may find
To honour him more than I honour some:
'Most beauteous cock', I'll say, and call to mind
How sweet that cock may make the honey come.
You know this cock, my love, for it is yours:
Yours to keep in, yours to let out of doors.

Each morning he would go to the door for the letters, and then come to the table again, his head down as he went over the words. Then he would go over them again, and again and again. There could be two such letters for him—more. Then, when my father had gone up, would be the time for him to show them to me.

One morning may go for many. He had gone to find the letters: two for him and one for me. I'll keep mine and look at it when I have more time. He'll tear in to his. Father's will come when the king's steward's men have had a look.

'Is she good to you?' I had to ask.

'She is.'

'And you: you are good to—'

'Have no fear.'

I had to say more, but what?

'You and I have not', I went on, 'been quite as—'

He raised a hand.

They do not love that do not show their love,
So should this love we have go on not seen?
You are my owl, my robin and my dove,
You are what is to come and what hath been.
I see you in the flowers upon the grass,
I see you when I think and when I pray,
I see you when I look in to a glass,
I see you as the sun and as the day.
You are my saint, so I in God believe;
My soul is in your hand, yours not to blame:
All that I ask is that you should receive
These gifts in which there never could be shame.
In my heart as in yours there is no doubt:
What reason then, my love, not to come out?

We went out and up the mountain, he and I.

He did not ask of me and my love. Never.

But he must see it. They must all see it.

12

O my honey, my love, o away up on the breath of a sigh we go, hey, as what is us rises in this light, out of the window and over the morning and over the day, and up steep to the light as the heels of heaven draw us, and us touching the sun with one hand, touching the light that is keen like joy on that one hand that comes from the two of us and we do not know which.

This is what it was, my heart, and this is what it will be.

As for now, I do not mind if it is day, if it is night.

Is the sun up? No. Then it must be night.

An owl will call to the night with grave music. A robin vows it is now morning, and bells the morning.

Night, day: there is no difference for me. What will make the difference is if you are with me.

We have been with each other in the night and in the day. You would find me at night and speak to me of your day. I would find you in the morning and tell you of my night. We would be givers to each other, givers of night and day.

What will truly make it day for me is you. It is night now, for you are not here. This is true night, this is what it is, without you, that are my sun.

You are my sun. You have sun-blasted me, and turned me to light.

You have made me like glass—like glass in an ecstasy from your light, like glass in which light rained and rained and rained and goes on, like glass in which there are showers of light that cannot end.

It is as if my hand, my arm, my shoulder, all of me is nothing now but this light.

you are the sun
your two eyes are the doors of the sun
and it is mine to be blown from the sun
and it is mine to be sucked in to the sun
light in light

We are two souls in one. They should see this. They should fear me. They should not know what it is that they have before their eyes. Their eyes should be jangled by me, by you in me, by the sun in me.

What reason do they have, then, to say nothing to me? What reason do they have to go on as if this—this light-being, this being of light—could still be me as I was?

They should have raised an arm over their eyes. They should have held their eyes from me, turned from me, not to look at the sun that is in me.

How may they be at table with the sun?

How may they speak of what clothes to wear for the morning when they have with them showers of light?

You have made me this.

This is the reason there's no difference of day from night. In the night I see by my own light, which is your light. Light falls from me, your light. And it falls without end, as it comes to me from you without end.

But then you are, as well, night. You are the sun and you are night. You draw light to the in-most of you. You take in light and it goes.

When you are with me, it is as if we are in a night that we have made, a night that you and I have made for us, a home of night in the day.

It is as if, where we are, there could be no other light but what we are: this light of two as one.

You come to me, and I have to find my way to you with my hand, touching you with my hand, in the profound night of you.

My eyes still see, but what they see means nothing. Nothing they see is true. What is true cannot be seen, for all that is true we may say in two words: my love. And this all we may say in another two words: your love. There is no difference. My love is your love, as I and you are one—one in the night that is us. There is nothing but us. There is nothing but love.

What was, in all of time, was us and love. What will come we do not fear, for it will come and we will know it: us and love.

We will make light of that day when we are wed: it is no more than one tomorrow, and we have many. The bells and the flowers and the music and the vows: these are all nothing. These go. We last.

Your hand is in my hand. My heart is in your heart.

we have one heart
to keep and restore us
from here to tomorrow
we call that heart love

And I may call it us. Us. This little one of my words, king of my words.

I say it again and again: it is sweet on my tongue. Us. Us. Us. I have to have more and more of it, and I may make more and more of it, when I wish and where I wish. Us. Us.

Us. I have had this honey with me for months, on my tongue and in my mind. To be away from you would end me, so I have you with me night and day, on my tongue. You and I to make us. Us. Us. Us.

'I' and 'me', we may let them go: they are words we may do without. They could be lost, for what could they be to us when we are lost in each other?

If we look now, as this 'us' rises to the heavens, at the things that have been 'I' and 'me', what do we see? Things that long for you—things that do not know you are never away. Letters blown over and shaking, waving in the light of the sun that we now are. Letters lost in the night that we are.

From when we made us, these words meant nothing. I do not believe in them. I believe in us.

Come here. Be here again with me. When you come, we will be here again. You will restore us.

Remember how it was when we dove down the ecstasy of the heavens to be with one another. We will do that again.

Be with me shoulder to shoulder, arm in arm, as we face what we must face. Be with me touching me.

Do you remember when we lay down in the grass on the brow of the mountain? My face is in that grass now. No-one but you could find me here. And you will find me. We will be here again, in the grass and the flowers.

a hand touching a hand becomes a rose
what the hand is touching becomes a rose
rose on rose, rose in rose, rose and rose
a rose that, shaking, rises as another rose

I did not know what I was before. I did not know I was meant to be one of two. I was lost and did not know the reason. Now I know. I took the lesson from you. Two are better than one.

You are my path, and you are with me on that path, hand in hand, and you find your path in me. Each of us treads on the other, but so light.

I will be where you are, and if you are there, so must I be. We cannot now be lost from each other.

And we are more. Look: we are a table, we are a green bed, we are a glass of violets at the window in the morning sun, we are a door out to the mountain, we are that mountain, we are all.

o green bed of green light
you loosed and composed me
your hand is a herb
your arm another
and these have held me as
I have gone on in the green chamber that is you

But I cannot tell you what I most wish to tell you, for there are no words for what I would say.

Could there, then, be music again? Could I sing to you, sing you? Could I take your face as my music lesson and sing?

May it be so. May you be music, for I will never find the words of you, for there are no such words.

How little they seem to me, the words that I have!

Love. Heart. You.

In my head they are rich and reckless, but as I speak them, each becomes a pale cast of what it was.

It could be that I should let words go.

as in a nō play
when a hand rises to speak
and will say nothing

But how should I do that when I know that you keep still so that I may speak? So I go on with these thoughts, which are all thoughts of you, for I have no thoughts but of you and no memory but of you—of you and for you.

All falls.

Other things have gone away.

I have tumbled head over heels down a mountain without end.

This love is harsh. It will draw me away from all that I was. It will, and not with a light hand, take me out from my home. It blasted the me they all know.

But then, it will make me over again, this love. It will show me what I was meant to be, which is us.

all before I bore gifts
keen I held them out in my hand
as one and another went by
now you have given me yours
and in your arm I see mine

We are at a table. We will be at this table to the end of all.

You play your king. I have lost. I love to have lost to you. Now your hand comes over the table.

You say: 'Give me your hand'.

13

Last night I made up my mind: I must go. Now indeed I have done what I could. Now I truly have done *all* I could.

And what was that? End something. Go over all there was up to now, restore it all to my mind one last time, and so end it. I *had* to do that, so it seemed. I had to come to an end before I could find the path to take on from here. I had to look again at what they had given me, all of it. I had to take it in my hand and shatter it, shatter the mould. I have come to see that my path up to now was a path made for me—and it could go on. I do not like it, and I will not take it. More and more I know where it goes.

I have to make another way. I have to find another way. And now I have the powers to do that. I could not do it without help. Help is here: the help I have, now that there is another with me—with me and in me, one that may see with my eyes and give with my hand. I know that what was me will have to come to an end, an end that I will have made. Not death! By no means. But this: I will have left that 'me' and gone.

Up to now my father and my brother have given me the reason I stayed, but the grace that I have seen come over my brother of late—that grace of love, which with him will come to be more—lets me think he could keep an eye on my father as well as I would. It was good, these last months, to see them find one another again a little. Now they may go on from here, and may do so all the better for my being away.

As for him, the young lord, there's no more I may do. I have been sucked in over-long, and I may have done him no good by that. Now he, as well, may find himself. Now he may take his play another way. I wish him well.

No doubt it will be more hard for me to let go of my brother and, most of all, my father—but not as hard as it would be to go on here, as a 'me' I now know to be false. It was not false before: it was right, and true, and good. But that's over. And I'll go without some fare-well speech. When I go from this home—a home that again now is no home to me, no more than the memory of a home—it will not be with a tear in my eye and a piteous look but with joy. And how could I have my father think the joy is at being gone from him?

The command I obey is love's, but it is, as well, mine. Love will be patient, but not for long. Love will look for tomorrow, but wish it here now. I will make my tomorrow now; I will go, in time that love's bended to my will—in love that time's bended to my will, in will that love's bended to my time.

But how should I tell my father, then? By letters? No. And I cannot tell my brother and ask him to speak for me, for that would be worse than nothing. So I have held my tongue with the two of them and come now to see another two—two that by their own love will, I hope, see the reason I have to go: the king and his lady. If I may say what I have to say to them, then they will know what to say to my father. Let my father see nothing of what I will be. I would wish him left with the memory of what I was—left to remember and to know I was what I was *for* him, and for that to be, in his mind, all of me.

I have come to their home, and have with me the things I wish to take: some remembrances of my father, a speech of his in his own hand, a glass that was one of my brother's gifts to me, some clothes.

I know that I will not see my father and brother again. For me to do so, they would have to go as well: each of them would have to look for another path, and I do not believe they will. I wish they would. But I cannot make them, for then the path would not be their path.

When I went from them, they did not look up from the letters they had before them on the table—things to which they had to give some perusal. I went down, my things in one hand. My father could do nothing but redeliver my 'Good morning' to me; my brother's thoughts must all have been with what was in his hand. Then they went on, each to himself more than to the other, lost in thoughts:

'I may not now remember what I call....'

'I would like to think we could have *A Little Night Music* again some time....'

I could go with a light heart. And I did.

One last time I went up the mountain—to where I had gone so long before with my brother time upon time, but now to think—and from there I have come here, to the king's. The watchman at the door, a pale young soldier in state green, was one I know, and he let me in before I had time to ask. I went from chamber to chamber to look for them, touching door upon door (for the lay-out I know), knocking for fear I would come upon them without their expectation of it—for fear, as well, I would come upon the young lord, which I had no wish to do—and at last I did find them. No other was with them. It's been the young lord's way, these last months, to keep to himself.

As I went in, before they could quite see me, I took a look at them. There they are. They face each other quite still, as if lost in doubt of one another. What *are* you? Where have we come from, we two? What have we done? But it could be that all this comes from my own thoughts, as I look at them. Then, as they see me, the doubt falls from each face and the king rises. He does seem quite better now.

'How good it is to see you! Come here to us and be *with* us! Good, good! Would you like something?'

At this he turned to his lady: 'My sweet, what do we have that would not speak woe of the king's table? Is there still some of what we had?'

She: 'The does' eyes?'

He: 'Indeed, the does' eyes.'

'Thank you, my lord, but no', I say. 'I had something at home. That's quite all right, my lord. Truly.'

'As you wish', from the king. 'So.'

It would seem he cannot think what to say, so it's over to the lady, and she goes right to what's on my mind—almost.

'Have you come here to speak of your father?'

I think what to say for a little time, and she goes on: 'It's so good to see him look so well now—is it not, my sweet? And no fear as to his....'

'Memory' (the king).

'Indeed, my sweet', the lady goes on again. 'And how is your good....' She cannot see where to lay down that glass.

'My brother, madam?' I say. 'He is well, madam.'

That would seem to draw an end to these little remembrances, and there is nothing more we have to say to one another. They cannot think what my reason could have been to come here. I, by now, wish I had never done so. But I see that I *must* do what I have come to do, and so I speak again.

'I have come to you on this cold morning to tell you that by the end of the day, when the sun goes down, I will have gone from here. Please do not speak of this to my father, and do not speak of it to my brother—not before I will be well away. I must ask that you do not let them know that I have gone—and gone for good, as it will be—before there could be no hope they would find me.'

The king, with one hand on his beard: 'Gone for good, you say?'

The lady, with one hand shaking in the other: 'Where, but where, my sweet love? And not with your father's wish? O no! No, no! Please, you have to obey! Do as you have been made to do! It is indeed cold out there. You must be here with us to the end! I had it in my heart that you would be the one to—'

But she is held by a look from the king and cannot go on. At that look she becomes cast down, and the effect on me is to make me think I must do something. I take the lady's arm and we go to the window. As we go, I say this: 'Madam, you must know what it's like for me here. Draw the lesson from your own words: obey, do as you have been made. Is that all there is to it? Do you not think—will it never have seemed to you—that we could find other words for what we are? What *reason* to obey? What *reason* to be patient and do what another will ask? What *reason* do you yourself have not to go?'

Whilst I speak she's turned to look at the king again, but we are at the window now, and I have my hand held out, and she cannot but look where I wish.

'Look at the powers before us,' I say, 'on the ground before us. Look down at them, on this morning of sun and turf and hope.'

'I do, I do.' And indeed the lady's eyes look keen.

'Look at them', I go on. 'What may we see? There is a holy father waving his hand. Over there a youth in a green shirt. And that little one by him that may be his brother, touching his brow as he rises now from the grass and lets go of the flowers he had held. A mountain soldier with a beard, and his daughter. Some men over there on their own: they seem lost. A scholar with a long face. They have all come. They do not know what for, but they have come: give them that. Their eyes are raised in expectation. They have stayed up all night for us, some of them. They look at us. They do not speak, for they have no words. Their *eyes* ask. What will this be? What will this be now?'

But, as we look, two do indeed speak—two we cannot see. Their words come to us, and I see the lady look up as well. They come as if from a long way away, and they are grave and profound, the words of watchmen. 'What goes there?' 'Nay,' the other answers, 'show yourself.'

They make me wish to go right away, these words. They seem like words come to receive me in to something I do not wish for. They seem like the words of vows I do not wish to make, and I let go of the lady's hand. But she, with eyes on what I show, cannot give mind to this.

'I see, I see!' She's turned to me. 'There's a bore out there with a look of your father!'

I shatter the glass.

They are gone now—they that had been no more

than a form on the glass, made of light. Cold comes in.

'See, lady! There's nothing there! Nothing and no-one! Out there snow falls!'

'No.... No....' She cannot look; she is shaking that not so noble head.

And then in no time at all she's with the king again, and they do something that was not at all in *my* expectation of how this morning would go: They sing. Indeed, they do—as if we could have music again, as if there was no reason not to. They sing as one, the king waving a one-two as they go: it's a right knees-up.

There's nothing I would not do
To have you with us here,
But it must be up to you:
These words are not to fear!
Alas, alas, death will come to us all,
But look: you'll have remembrance in the grave!

'You cannot play with me', I say. 'For me that's all over. What comes now I do not know.'

Then, out of no where, I go up to the lady and say this:

There was a time when I held you to be
One I could some day tell my in-most heart,
But now I know that day will never come:
The light is on but there's no-one at home.

But I do not wish to speak thus. It's as if she will draw me in, and I have to come away again to the window and close my eyes so that I may go on with what I *wish* to say: 'But this I *do* know: that what comes will be mine and will be true.'

The king lets go of his lady and comes up to me.

'What is true?'

Before I could say something, he's turned to his lady: 'My sweet, would you let us have some words, O and I, one on one? Thank you.'

The lady goes, and his eyes are on me again when the words of the two watchmen come another time. 'What goes there?' 'Nay, show yourself.' I look hard at the king. He's given nothing away, but I know, as truly as I may see him, that the two watchmen did speak again. Their words make me fear the more. This is the time to go. This is the time when I *must* go. Another night here and the time will be over.

'Do you not like it here?'

'This was my home, my lord, as you know. That's all there is to say. For each of us there comes a day when home, where we have been raised, becomes something *to* which and *in* which we are locked. For many that will be all well and good. But not for me. I find I now have in my hand a key.'

'I think I know him.'

'The key, my lord, is not a he and not a she—which is not to say that love may not be a help.'

'You cannot love and still be here with us?'

His hand is on my wrist. His speech is like a sigh.

'You cannot love—no, my little fair one—you cannot love that youth of my lady's—that lady the two of us have had, my brother and me, one before the other—if not the two at one time. Ha! Think of that!'

His hand now comes up my arm as he goes on.

'If I did, before all this, take some joy in this lady, that day is done—and that night long, long done. I took the lady for reason of state. Are you with me?'

'My lord,' I say, 'all I have come here for is to tell you I must go. You cannot say me nay. What I would ask is for you to speak with my father. Tell him I go on my own, and of my own will. Tell him my mind is made up, as never before. Tell him I know what I face. Tell him I love him, and could never have left if I did not have to. I know how he'll be, but some words from you would be a help.'

'I would have you wish for more—and not for your father but for yourself. Then I would give you more and more and more.'

His hand is on my shoulder, his breath on my face.

'I think, my lord, that I had better go right away.'

Now he's turned from me, and there's a difference in his speech, which comes at me like an oath—harsh, blown.

'You speak of nothing but yourself, to no-one but yourself. You'll never find the one you look for: he's no more than a play of thoughts in your mind. But we cannot tell you this, for some reason. You *will* not take it from us.

'You think you may come here and tell me of *love*'—God, let me not remember the face he made at this! —'Take a good look at yourself. See if what you think is love is not something you could have better right here.

'You are a poor little lost soul', he goes on. 'You will go out from here and you will find nothing, nothing, nothing, for there is nothing out there for you to find. We are all there is. There is no other *way* you may look for. There is no heaven out there made for you.'

'Be it heaven, be it hell', I say, 'I *will* find it.'

I know I have to keep my eyes on his; I cannot look away.

'Go then. There'll be no remembrance of you here. It will be as if you had never been. The effect of O.'

But now I have turned to go.

I say no more. I have left that chamber of horrors. All I have to do now is find the way by which I had come in, but one does not have to look long for a door—not if a door is what one would wish for more than all other things.

Look: the door is here, where my hand is.

Look: my hand is on the door.

And look: I have gone out.

14

I go out now. I let go of the door, and do not look to see my hand as I take it away.

Snow falls. So: I will go on in the snow. I have my hope with me, and a staff in my hand.

I look up, as if I could see the snow as it falls, as if I could keep my eye on a little of it and see it come down, all the way to the ground.

I cannot. The snow flowers are all like each other, and I cannot keep my eyes on one. I have given up and gone on.

All like each other as well are my treads over the snow, for here, some way on, I have stayed and turned to look at them. In each of them there is now more snow—more in the treads some way away than in these here that I was in before I turned. The snow comes to white them over—white me over. It will take away each mark I made, will take away the memory of my path, so that, when I have gone right away, there will be nothing to see of me and my path. Before long all memory of me will be gone. *I* will be gone.

Now I have turned to face again where I must go.

There is light on the snow still. And there is light *in* the snow. All is still. There is nothing to call to me, no mark to show me the way. There is no-one to speak—no-one but me, and I do not speak. There is nothing. All is white.

I look again the other way, to see the mountain I must have come over. But I cannot see a mountain. All I see is snow, nothing but snow—snow and my treads, which will go in the snow.

Before me—for now I have turned again to look

where I must go on—there is more snow. Snow falls over all that was here before, over all that was in my mind. I will have to find how to think again, believe again, know again. The little that is left to me is me: with that I will go on.

It is not as cold as it seemed when I was with the king and his lady. But memory is pale. It means little. It means nothing.

Will is more: my will to be here, in the majesty of the morning, where all is turned to white, where all goes to white—all but me.

Snow. Now. No. O.

This is me, the one that goes on in the snow, which she will mark as she treads, for a little time, and then be gone. What is other becomes white and without feature. She goes on.

I go on in this white: white to make me know what white is. I go on. It is not that I must but that I will. I will go on.

But I could will it another way.

Now I must make up my mind. I take one last look at where I have come from. They will all be there still: my father, my brother, him, the king, his lady. I could go over my treads again before the snow falls quite over them: they still mark the way.

Him. Could I still do something for him that would make a difference? Could I take him by the hand so that, when it comes, I held him from what must be?

The more I have come away, the better I see what I have left, and it becomes like another's memory. Here in the snow I see there was nothing I could do. I was one of his play things.

But it does not have to be like that. Now—with

what I know now, and the powers I have—I could make a difference. I could go again to him, and the words would come to me. It could all be turned. And no-one but me could do it. Is that not, then, what I should do?

Now I look the other way, to the unbraced white. I could go on to more of that white.

I could go again over my treads to where I have come from. This time I could make things better for him. I know I could. It does not have to go as they say.

I could do that: go home and not go on.

I could go on, and find what I still do not know.

This way, that way.

I have stayed here to think, and then:

I choose.

Other titles in print from Reality Street Editions:

Poetry series

Tony Baker: *In Transit,* £7.50
Nicole Brossard: *Typhon Dru,* £5.50
Cris Cheek/Sianed Jones: *Songs From Navigation*, £12.50
Kelvin Corcoran: *Lyric Lyric,* £5.99
Ken Edwards: *eight + six*, £7.50
Allen Fisher: *Dispossession and Cure*, £6.50
Allen Fisher: *Place*, £18
Susan Gevirtz: *Taken Place*, £6.50
Jeff Hilson: *stretchers*, £7.50
Jeff Hilson (ed.): *The Reality Street Book of Sonnets*, £15
Anselm Hollo (ed. & tr.): *Five From Finland,* £7.50
Allan Kolski Horwitz & Ken Edwards (ed.) *Botsotso*, £12.50
Fanny Howe: *O'Clock*, £6.50
Peter Jaeger: *Rapid Eye Movement*, £9
Tony Lopez: *Data Shadow,* £6.50
David Miller: *Spiritual Letters (I-II)*, £6.50
Redell Olsen: *Secure Portable Space*, £7.50
Maggie O'Sullivan: *In the House of the Shaman*, £6.50
Maggie O'Sullivan: *Body of Work,* £15
Maggie O'Sullivan (ed.): *Out of Everywhere,* £12.50
Sarah Riggs: *chain of minuscule decisions in the form of a feeling,* £7.50
Denise Riley, *Selected Poems*, £9
Peter Riley: *Excavations*, £9
Lisa Robertson: *Debbie: an Epic*, £7.50*
Lisa Robertson: *The Weather*, £7.50*
Maurice Scully: *Steps*, £6.50
Maurice Scully: *Sonata*, £8.50
Robert Sheppard: *The Lores,* £7.50
Lawrence Upton: *Wire Sculptures*, £5
Carol Watts: *Wrack*, £7.50

* co-published with New Star Books, Vancouver, BC

4Packs series

1: *Sleight of Foot* (M Champion, H Kidd, H Tarlo, S Thurston), £5
2: *Vital Movement* (A Brown, J Chalmers, M Higgins, I Lightman), £5
3: *New Tonal Language* (P Farrell, S Matthews, S Perril, K Sutherland), £5
4: *Renga+* (G Barker, E James/P Manson, C Kennedy), £5

Narrative series
Ken Edwards: *Futures*, £6.99
Ken Edwards: *Nostalgia for Unknown Cities*, £8.50
John Hall: *Apricot Pages*, £6.50
David Miller: *The Dorothy and Benno Stories*, £7.50
Douglas Oliver: *Whisper 'Louise'*, £15

Reality Street Editions depends for its continuing existence on the Reality Street Supporters scheme. For details of how to become a Reality Street Supporter, or to be put on the mailing list for news of forthcoming publications, write to the address on the reverse of the title page, or email **info@realitystreet.co.uk**

Visit our website at: **www.realitystreet.co.uk**

Reality Street Supporters who have sponsored this book:

David Annwn
Andrew Brewerton
Paul Buck
Clive Bush
John Cayley
Adrian Clarke
Ian Davidson
Mark Dickinson
Allen Fisher/Spanner
Sarah Gall
Chris Goode
Giles Goodland
Catherine Hales
John Hall
Alan Halsey
Robert Hampson
Jeff Hilson
Peter Jaeger
L Kiew
Peter Larkin
Tony Lopez
Ian McMillan
Michael Mann
Peter Manson
Deborah Meadows
Peter Middleton
Geraldine Monk
Marjorie Perloff
Pete & Lyn
Tom Quale
Peter Quartermain
Josh Robinson
Will Rowe
Anthony Rudolf
Barry Schwabsky
Maurice Scully
Julius Smit
Hazel Smith
Andrew Taylor
Tony Trehy
Keith Tuma
Lawrence Upton
Catherine Wagner
Sam Ward
John Welch/Many Press
Susan Wheeler
John Wilkinson
Tim Woods
+ 4 anonymous